I am Stefan Stahl

C. Craig R. McNeil

Published by Craig McNeil, 2023.

This is a work of fiction. Similarities to real people, places, or events are entirely coincidental.

I AM STEFAN STAHL

First edition. November 13, 2023.

ISBN: 979-8215705193

Written by C. Craig R. McNeil.

Also by C. Craig R. McNeil

An Atlantean Triumvirate
An Atlantean Triumvirate
Ghosts of the Past
The Centre Cannot Hold

Terra Inferus
The Pillars of Britain
Foundations of the Reich
Cracks in the Pillars

Standalone
I am Stefan Stahl

Prisoner 50

The prisoner's shouting, swearing and cursing was clearly audible from all the way down the corridor as he was brought up from the holding cells. Despite his advancing years, the big man was putting up an almighty struggle, gamely resisting the wide leather straps that bound his ankles, knees and wrists as the four guards struggled to keep him flat on the trolley they had wheeled him in on.

Voss sighed wearily as he glanced at the clock that was fixed high up on the bare off-white wall of Room 249. As he watched, the minutes digit flipped over to 15. 1815 hours. The seconds digits continued their relentlessly slow flick, flick, flick. The date of 11th October 1984 stayed rigidly unmoving. The date never ceased to inspire a glimmer of hope within him. Someone hadn't replaced the clock with one showing the new date system, a small act of protest that would have been abruptly dealt with if the state bureaucracy ever found out. With a start he realised that the clock had sat on the wall for a long time now and no one had removed it, in fact no one had ever mentioned it, not even the guards. Small protests, tiny rebellions.

Only fifteen minutes to go before his shift in this godforsaken place ended. It had seemed to him that he could watch the clock for an hour at a time before the minutes number increased. It had been a long day, just one of many this week.

"Mein Gott! Will you please gag him!" Voss snapped to the guards who happily complied by viciously strapping a gag across the prisoner's mouth but not before two had yelped in pain after receiving nasty bites. The man was an animal, probably the reason why he was here today.

Prisoner number 50, thankfully the last one to be dealt with at the end of this exhausting day.

"Lift him onto the table," ordered Voss as he tapped some keys on his computer and called up the prisoner's mental profile, topographical brain scan, electrical brain scan, skull measurements, the usual. Ja gut, nothing out of the ordinary. All was well.

Voss jumped as metal crescent restraints snapped and clicked into place around the prisoner's limbs and torso. The guards stood back, wiping away sweat from their foreheads and nursing injured digits.

He sighed to himself, trying not to give into the mental torture he put himself through with every prisoner that had been brought to him today but he couldn't stop his eyes being drawn inexorably to the man's name. Every man he had killed today, every man he had murdered yesterday and the day before and the day before that, he had read their name and muttered quietly a small prayer for every one of them despite the risk of being overheard. Only the bleak and uncomforting state sanctioned religion of the Nazi State was allowed after all. Heil Hitler!

Oh. Voss paused, eyes narrowed as he leant into the computer screen, the green text casting a cadaverous glow on to his face. The prisoner had no name or rather it was shown as 'Classified'. Most unusual. Voss wondered if the man was a member of the Resistance. He cast a glance over at the figure heaving futilely against the restraints, noting the limbs that although still powerful were wasted by age and the deep wrinkles on the man's exposed face. Nein, he was too old by far.

"Is there a problem Voss?" asked one of the guards impatiently. "Can we get this last one vaped now so we can hand over to the next shift?"

"Nein, no problem. No problem at all," muttered Voss. The next shift took over at 1830 on the dot. He could hear the clatter of footsteps in the outside corridors as everyone moved to stand by the door to their windowless rooms to immediately take over from those leaving. It was 1823 now. Time enough to perform the procedure. His eyes fell to the date again, that small act of rebellion and he felts embers burn and spark to life within him.

He walked over to the prisoner, avoiding the man's eyes which followed his every move and lifted the delicate mesh of the engram device before placing it carefully and gently over the prisoner's bald head. The unknown man had stopped struggling, finally accepting the immutability of his fate. Voss gently placed his hand on the man's shoulder and looked into his eyes trying to communicate his plan via strength of thought. He could do no more with the guards still impatiently waiting to return the body. Voss pressed a green switch on the console next to the table. There was no discernible effect but the prisoner's eyes slowly closed as his being was drained from his biological mind and implanted into a engram storage chip. Voss had often wondered what was being done with the engram chips. Rumours had that they were being used to power new weapons somehow but then everything that was created in the name of scientific progress was used to power new weapons. It seemed to him that the only reason the Nazi State existed was to create new weapons to subjugate Earth's population.

A beep announced the completion of the task and Voss disconnected the husk from the engram machine and lifted the chip from its perch leaving the guards to pull the body off the table, onto the trolley and take it to the incinerators.

1829.

Voss quickly plugged the engram chip into his computer and verified the transfer had been completed successfully. His finger hovered over the button that said "Start Lobotomising Procedure".

1829, 25 seconds, 11th October 1984. He unplugged the chip and pushed it into the plastic tray where the other forty nine chips sat. One of many yet different now.

The shift change alarm blared stridently, shrill and headache inducing. Quickly Voss popped a cover on the plastic tray, ticked the checkboxes on his forms and walked out, giving only a brief auf wiedersehen to the new shift worker. The fire within was watered by nervousness, drowned in the sea of dull grey and harsh lights that formed the corridor to the locker rooms, quenched forever by the sight of the iron skies and bleak skyscraping tower blocks crowned by the ever present red, white and black flags of the Nazi Reich.

But Voss's small act of rebellion was remembered by the unchained personality locked away in the engram chip. Remembered for decades.

Neu Erde

Ich bin Stefan Stahl. I am twenty years old. I have been a member of the Nazi Party for as long as I can remember. After all I was born and raised in Munich, administrative centre of Bavaria and the beating heart of the Nazi Party in Deutschland.

I joined the SS when I was fifteen. I was tall for my age and I was not questioned too closely about the slight alteration I'd carefully made to my birthdate on my official papers. It was about the proudest moment of my life when I donned the night black uniform of the SS with the two lightning bolts on my lapel.

As anyone would expect from the superior German military, the training was rigorous and intense. I enjoyed the physical challenges immensely; sports at school had always been a favourite of mine. I came top in the live target shooting competition. It was fun but not as hysterically funny as some of my fellow trainees seemed to think.

Gruppenführer Hassgard must have seen potential in me. I always liked him. He was a stern man with a scarred face, always firm but fair. When some slaves were caught stealing food, he allowed them two minutes to say goodbye to their families before he set his dogs on the thieves. The families were used for target practice. Being shot is a quicker death than being savaged by dogs. It was said that one of the children even got away. It would not surprise me as they are smaller, more difficult targets to hit. So, ja, firm but fair.

I was called into his office one day, along with eight others I did not recognise, where we were told that we nine would be formed in to a special unit. We were not told what sort of special unit, only that we were being transferred immediately to a special project. A special unit for a special project... and one Der Fuhrer deemed of significant importance! However, along with several of my fellow new unit members, I was slightly suspicious. I had heard of some special units whose only duty was to guard facilities of importance to the Reich. A vital duty of course but I wanted action, I wanted to face the Reich's enemies and throw them back into the Deutsch Sea!

As I said, we left immediately, leaving our training camp in a transport truck with our uniforms and meagre belongings stuffed in canvas bags. The journey was long, the benches uncomfortable, but we of the SS do not complain. I would have liked to have seen where we were going but the rear flap was pulled down and tightly secured. I stripped down my Schmeisser and oiled and greased all the parts before carefully slotting them back together. By now I can do such a task in my sleep but I wished to stave off the boredom. Some of my comrades did likewise, one read a heavily thumbed copy of Mein Kampf, some talked quietly amongst themselves, one slept.

I was curious as to our destination. The heavy canvas cover blocked out much of the light from outside but it seemed to me that we were travelling north on a road with little in the way of traffic. The Autobahn I thought given how smooth the ride was. As we neared what I now realise to be the end of our journey, we left the Autobahn and travelled along a far rougher and bumpier road which sloped upwards. The air became cooler and I guessed we were driving up a mountain track.

By the time we stopped, it was night. It was so dark that when the rear flap was raised none of us could see anything - no shadowy outlines of whoever had opened the flap, no road beyond, not even our own hands in front of our faces. I could hear movement though. I could hear a metal tread on stone, and loud raspy breathing. Suddenly, spotlights blazed on, blinding me with their dazzling brightness and temporarily obscuring the figure at the rear of the truck.

As my eyes adjusted, I could not help but gasp when I saw the supersoldier standing there. He, or it, was enormous, even by supersoldier standards, and filled the canvas aperture with his bulk and height. I was surprised to see that he was not bare chested. In the barracks, it was said that the supersoldiers were made bare chested and that they bolted on pieces of metal and armour directly on to their

I AM STEFAN STAHL

grey and heavily scarred flesh. This one was encased in armour from the neck down. His face lacked the brutishness of the supersoldiers and was pale rather than the usual grey pallor. A stark white even. What struck me was just how human it appeared, missing the Negroid features that I'd been led to believe was prevalent amongst the supersoldiers.

On the supersoldier's left shoulder armour, I saw the stark, simple emblem of Nazi Germany. I felt my chest swell with pride when I saw it. However, on the left breast were the two jagged lightning bolts of my parent organisation, the SS, under which was a skull and crossbones and at this, my eyes narrowed and my heart beat faster in anger. The SS set the example for Germanic racial purity. Why was this beast allowed to wear the symbol of the epitome of the German race? I kept my unrest to myself.

"Get out," the supersoldier said to us in a harsh metallic voice. So we got out.

I had guessed correctly. We were high in the mountains, the peaks of which stood as jagged ebony against the stars spread across the sky like dust. The cold bit deeply once we were away from the warm confines of the truck. Further spotlights clicked on and shone down on us as we followed our giant guide until he stopped seemingly at random. I could not see beyond the glare of the lights so I was startled by the sudden appearance of a man in a SS officers uniform. The nine of us clicked our heels together and saluted smartly, even more so when we saw the silver oak leafs on his lapels - a gruppenführer no less! He was a undistinguished man of average height, clean shaven of course with an unremarkable face though his eyes seemed to bore straight through me - they appeared to glow in the harsh light that flooded where we stood.

"Guten abend," he said with a soft accent I could not place. "You men have been chosen by your commandant as the very best of his trainees. Here at Schloss Schwabenstein we will make you even better. We will mould you into supreme warriors worthy of the SS."

I remember his voice being flat and emotionless. I had the impression the Gruppenführer was bored as if he had made this speech many times before. All the while he talked, he walked up the line looking at us. No - **examining** us. As he paused in front of me, I noticed his smell. He smelt of dust and antiseptic. He wore no cologne nor was there a hint of the sharp tang of sweat. He did not smell human.

His name is SS-Gruppenführer Doktor Jaegerstass and he is the kommandant of this research facility at Schloss Schwabenstein. I feel he is a great man, a man of great vision and drive, even a future leader of the Reich, though I keep such a blasphemous though to myself. Men greater than I have been executed for less.

We are all proud participants in an übermensch programme. Gruppenführer Jaegerstass says there are many übermensch programmes in the Reich and beyond but that his is the most advanced and sophisticated. The Thousand Year Reich has many enemies and great as the soldiers of the SS and even the Wehrmacht are, they cannot be everywhere nor can they stand against the insurmountable odds of the combined forces of the British and their heathen Bolshevik allies. The Gruppenführer says he takes the best of the SS and makes us better. I am curious as to how he will achieve this. We are all superbly fit, excellent marksmen with an equally excellent understanding of squad tactics. From my brief conversations with the eight who came with me (we have been billeted in separate dormitory cells) we were all in line for promotion to feldwebel.

I am very fed up. In the past few days I have been poked, prodded and jabbed more times than I have ever been in my entire life. I've had blood samples taken from me, I've given skin samples, taken and repeated many reaction tests, sat intelligence tests, been injected with fluids containing the Fuhrer only knows what, and sat more tests. I am a soldier of the Reich. I should be at the front line fighting for the Third Reich and Der Fuhrer. I am trying to be patient but I am finding it extremely difficult to keep my frustration under control. I am angry all the time, my rage a furnace, nein..., a volcano that threatens to explode at the slightest mishap. Nothing is explained to us, no reasons are given despite our enquiries. We are drip fed liquids (instead of information) while lying on bare metal tables in a clinically scented ward. Why there is a hospital ward in the schloss, I of course, do not know. Gruppenführer Jaegerstass frequents a room next to the ward, separated from it by a glass wall. His face is a dispassionate mask at all times. My table faces the glass wall so I can see him checking dials and writing notes on a clipboard. Sometimes he is accompanied by masked and helmeted supersoldiers.

I feel very well this morning. I have not slept yet I am as alert as if I have had a good nights sleep. I feel... gut. It is difficult to explain as I do not have the words, the vocabulary. I am strong. I feel fit. My pulse is very slow and it feels as if my heart only beats ten times a minute. I must be wrong about that though I feel I could run a hundred miles with ease, lift a Tiger tank over my head then run a hundred miles more. Everything I see appears to be sharp and clear with bright and vivid colours and the patterns and textures on the stones in my cell surprise me with their intricateness. How have I not noticed them before?

We have been told that today will be the last day of the übermensch programme. I am greatly relieved. The forced isolation and the lack of contact with anyone has been surprisingly wearying. I wonder if we will be split between individual units or if we will be kept together.

I must go now.

I do not remember much about the procedure I underwent. I was led, along with five others, in to what appeared to be yet another rectangular hospital ward except that it was very sparse with only three beds against each of two opposing walls, each bed separated from the other by drawn curtains. I write 'beds' but 'tables' would be a better description. I noted with some alarm that each bed had restraining straps, a fact that did not go unnoticed by my companions either. Our glances to each other must have been noticed as a masked medical orderly dressed in light blue marched up and assured us that the restraints were for our own safety. As he finished, a familiar voice crackled from hidden speakers. I had missed it entirely on entering the ward but was not surprised to find a long glass window at one end through which General Doctor Jaegerstass looked down on us, a mouthpiece in his hand.

"Soldiers of the Reich," he said, "Do not be afraid. The procedure you are undergoing is incredibly delicate. So delicate that if you moved even one single millimetre during the operation then you would die."

He paused to let his words sink in and sink in they did. I became truly afraid. I did not wish to die on an operating table as the end result of a mad man's folly! I have much respect for the General Doctor but his ideas are strange and far fetched.

"I ask for your time, your patience, but above all, your courage," he continued, "And for that I will guarantee that when you are revived from your procedure that you will be an Aryan god, truly an übermensch to be feared by the enemies of the Reich."

Whether it was the loudspeakers or the man himself, the speech was delivered in a flat and emotionless tone that did little to allay my fears. Yet I was not prepared to lose face in front of my fellow SS. I stepped forward and was immediately directed to a bed where I found a medical orderly standing next to a small movable table. He directed me to lie on the bed (I remember it being very cold) and proceeded to strap me in. The straps were made of thick leather with heavy metal buckles. I did not find the straps attached to my limbs too uncomfortable but when the last one was placed over my forehead and tightened, I felt a terrible sense of claustrophobia as I was unable to move in any way at all. Out of the corner of my eye, I saw the medical orderly silently signal in the direction of the glass window before nodding and turning to tend to something out of sight. I could hear the tinkle and delicate clatter of things being moved about on the table before the orderly turned to face me with a syringe full of bright blue fluid. Before I could ask what it was, he leaned forward and injected me in my forearm. At this point, my memory of events becomes fuzzy. I can only recall that the injection stung and that the stinging sensation quickly spread from my forearm to my fingers and then swiftly up to my shoulder before spreading to the rest of my body. Suddenly I could not see. It was as if a light switch had been thrown such was the suddenness of the darkness. My hearing started to fade as well. The last thing I remember hearing was the buzz of an electric saw and the whining of a drill followed by a man screaming in agony. At the time I thought it may have been me screaming but then darkness descended in its entirety and I could not tell.

Ich bin Stefan Stahl. I am two days old. My official designation is 1-2-5; cohort leader of second cohort, unit five.

This is the first time I have been able to write in my journal for several days. I do not know why I still keep this record. It does not feel right. My brain rebels at the thought of picking up a pen and writing yet once I break through this barrier, I find it oddly comforting; a reminder of my past as a flesh and blood human being. It took me several attempts to pick up the pen as these new fingers I have are big and clumsy. The metal tips are slippery and I have little doubt that they were not designed to grasp small items such as pens. The price for my increased warrior prowess is my current inability to do the small things I used to take for granted. For example I can no longer eat with a knife and fork like a civilised German. It is much to my chagrin that I am forced to use a large spoon to scoop up my nutritional gruel from the bowl. My comrades do not seem particularly bothered by this inconvenience. I shall adapt.

As I read back what I have written above I surprise myself by seeing that I have focussed on such a mundanity. I am a warrior of the Reich, one of a new generation and I write about not being able to eat properly! A thought flashes to the forefront that I will not need to eat much longer. This troubles me. Is it a premonition of my death or something else?

When I arrived here at Schloss Schwabenstein, I measured 1.75 metres in height. I was a fine physical specimen of manhood able to run twenty kilometres in full battle dress before breakfast. My wife had already been chosen for me from the SS breeding programme.

Now I have to stoop to pass through doorways that are two and a half metres high. In some of the older parts of the schloss, I need to walk sideways, like a crab. I am... I think I am barely human anymore. I don't think I will be allocated a wife. My body is now all metal - I live in an armoured shell. I think. I do not know if my body of bone and flesh is encased in this shell or if what I can see is me. I flex my hands and stretch my arms wide. They do not feel like an extension of me - they feel like they **are** me. I tried to wriggle my toes but I don't appear to have toes anymore, just hoof like appendages.

I am a Stürmgard according to Gruppenführer Doktor Jaegerstass. My thoughts go back to when I first arrived at the schloss and faced one of my fellow Stürmgard and my concern at him (or it) wearing the symbol of the SS. I am troubled that I am now a Stürmgard myself. Purity of race, purity of blood, purity of thought - I have a terrible feeling that I am left with just my thoughts. Perhaps I have been purified beyond considerations of race and blood. I cling to that hope as laughter echoes in my head. I fear even my mind has been contaminated. I hear voices.

The past few days have shown me sights I still cannot believe. I will start from the beginning, where all sehr gut stories start.

My unit is Weiss, Braun, Beckenbauer, Neuer, Durm, Müller, Jansen and Kruse; they are numbers two to eight. Although I was unsure of their names before, I now have no doubts. When I think of them, their names instantly spring to mind. Their faces, unnaturally small given the bulky proportions of their armour, are pale, blank and expressionless.

Inhuman I would venture, an attempt to transplant comforting visages onto killing machines.

We are all alike. Nein, that is wrong. We are identical. Identical save for our plastic faces and even they are hidden behind our visors when we go into battle. Our unit insignia of a skull in front of a lightning bolt (though it could be the lightning bolt is piercing the skull) and our unit numbers are painted on our shoulders and backs - there would be no way to identify ourselves without them.

I am a soldier of the Stürmgard. I know there are few, if any, that can equal me, yet my hand trembles as I contemplate the knowledge that I may have to return to those barren wastes to correct a horrific mistake.

I have taken a moment to gather my thoughts as I was greatly running ahead of myself. My cell is quiet, peaceful, the silence between the thick castle walls a welcoming relief to the constant howling wind that I have endured in the recent few days. So I begin again.

On the fourth day after I was reborn, I was taken along with my cohort down to the castle depths. I was surprised at how deep we went, certainly we descended far, far past the dungeon levels as the relatively smooth castle walls changed abruptly to roughly hewn rock. No one ever said anything. We did (and do) not communicate except to abruptly give and acknowledge orders. The silence between my cohort, between everyone, felt uncomfortable to me but no one else appeared to mind nor notice.

The noise of machinery could be heard long before we saw it. The unseen machinery pulsed and hummed with an unchanging rhythm like a heartbeat. If I could still feel my feet I have little doubt that I would have felt the vibrations long before I heard it.

Suddenly the path downwards ended and we passed through an archway and entered an enormous chamber. For a second my vision blacked out as my secondary eyelids (I had no idea I had secondary eyelids until now. Where did this knowledge come from? How did I get them?) automatically flicked down to protect my eyes from the sun that blazed in the centre of the cavern above a raised circular dais. As my vision restored itself by increments, I saw that the centre of the "sun" was a grey nothingness that swirled slowly like thick opaque fog. The intense light came from the jagged metal construction that surrounded the void; electrical bolts curled around the edifice like blue-white snakes. On occasion, thunder would boom and echo and re-echo around the cavern, drowning out the crackle of barely constrained electricity and the deep, deep hum of the Krystal powered generators that sat at the cavern side. Rainbows bathed the generators, the colours leaking out from the Krystal shards connected to the clumsy machines.

We stood on a large balcony half way up the cavern wall. The balcony was big enough for us all to gather without constraint. My comrades did not seem to display any interest in the hive of activity below them staring quite woodenly ahead. As I stared down at the grey void, somehow I knew that it was a portal, either a demonic creation or one derived from technological feats. While I watched, a convoy of half tracks appeared from the centre of the grey, engines chugging as they slowly rolled down the shallow slope. They were heavily laden with what I thought to be a combination of metal scrap and large crates. One carried wounded soldiers, some in stretchers, some barely standing, all exhausted and swathed in bloody bandages.

A wide staircase followed the curve of the wall down to the cavern floor. We were not slow in our descent, sparks flying from our shod hooves as we sped down the steps. I felt an eagerness for battle quicken within me, a need to grasp our waiting weapons from where they lay on a flatbed truck and to hurl ourselves in to the fray. Only my tempered SS will allowed me to maintain control of myself.

Surrounding the portal were bunkers of concrete and sandbags from which pointed heavy machine guns and cannon. But by now these were of little interest to me. Without pausing, I picked up my gun, a MG47 triple barrelled 2.5cm variant, and barked my orders to my cohort. I knew what was required of me, I knew what was beyond the grey swirls, I knew that even in my current übermensch state of being that I might not survive. But it did not matter. For the Reich, for the Aryan race and for Der Fuhrer I raced up the ramp, my cohort fanning out behind me like an arrowhead aimed at the heart of the Reich's enemies and we entered the portal.

When I was a child, my mother and father took me to a Nazi Party rally at Ingolstadt. It was a small affair with only a few hundred people in attendance, all wearing Party badges on their lapels, some with red armbands of the Party on their left arms. A few local Party grandees made suitably inspiring speeches about racial purity, the greed of the Jews and the greatness of Der Fuhrer's vision. I had heard such platitudes and denouncements before and was quite bored despite the cheering and applause that greeted them. I could also smell the bratwurst and whole pigs being cooked over a fire to feed the attendees, probably the main reason many people were there. I remember my mouth watering profusely at the delicious smells and wishing that the speeches would quickly be over with so I could run over for a plate of that wonderful food.

The fog came on us quickly and silently, muffling sounds so that I thought I was going deaf, a thought that panicked me greatly as I did not want to go to the special school that no one ever left. But what I remember most of all is the thickness of the heavy mist. Meine mutter held my hand tightly which was a strange sensation as I could not see her nor my hand. All I could see was swirling grey and sparkling white specks where water droplets caught the light. My eyes felt strange as I was unable to focus on the shifting cloud. The reason I mention this is that I was reminded of this fog when I entered the portal, a flashback that lasted a second as I dealt with the unnerving sensory deprivation. I maintained my headlong rush forward even though I had a feeling that I was not quite there, that I did not exist except as a disconnected consciousness. As I say, a strange feeling.

Neu Erde it was called. Whether the name was dreamed up either in haste or parody, I do not know but it looked nothing like the blue, green and white world of home. The wind screamed and howled through shredded clouds, the sun a cold two dimensional circle stuck on the uniformly iron sky. I felt elation at the familiar and comforting sight of the bright red flag of the Reich snapping in the wind from a flagpole on a rampart ahead of me.

I stood on top of the a ramp, which was the reverse of the one on the opposite side of the portal, slightly disorientated by the transition. The equipment surrounding us was identical though it was housed in squat, brutal concrete bunkers that had one side open to the portal to allow the necessary cables to tumble out on their way to the portal frame. Surrounding us stood the walls of the prefabricated Reichesfort, as grey as the sky. The fort was deserted save for a smattering of soldiers frantically raising wooden props against the gates directly in front of me, and another smattering on the ramparts. The fort was under attack. My squad appeared behind me one by one in quick succession. I directed them forward, ordering Durm and Kruse onto the ramparts on either side of the battered gate to support the Waffen SS who were firing on whoever was attacking. It sounded like a battering ram was being deployed, a hunch that was proven true when the left gate crashed back off its hinges, the thick beam set across it splintering in two and cleanly decapitating one of the soldiers behind it. Even as the twitching body fell to the ground in a red fountain of blood, the gate continued its fall and landed on two more soldiers. I heard them scream as I leapt forward to engage the enemy.

My strategy may appear foolhardy but I did not think the mutations (this was the first time I knew of the mutations. More would be revealed later) would expect such a rapid counter attack. I saw the corpulent throng surge forward even as the thick concrete ram was drawn back for a final blow. The ram heaved forward over the heads of the mutations before jarring to a dead stop as I caught the rounded front in my right hand. I pushed back, feeling the massive post crunch against two particularly large mutations who collapsed screaming and flailing as black blood spilled from their mouths and crushed chests. The battering ram frame collapsed and the ram fell on the two things ending their squeals. The mob quailed at the sight of me as they realised they faced a far greater threat than they had anticipated. Durm and Kruse opened up during the momentary pause and, as if it were a signal, so did I. I swung my gun around in an arc, the three barrels glowing red as they spat out their leaden death. It could only have been a minute but it seemed like an eternity of gunfire, flickering staccato gun flame and the slap of ripped wet meat falling on to the powdery grey ground.

Sometime after the battle, as we cleared away the bodies of the fallen; the mutations dumped into a hastily dug pit and burned, our own dead laid out on boards to be taken away through the portal, a convoy of vehicles arrived at the Reichesfort. The grey collection of half track troop carriers and similarly half tracked flat bed trucks rumbled up to the portal as the four towering robotic automata providing the rearguard clanked to a halt, two on either side of the gate. The trucks were laden with more strange technology for our scientists to pore over and use to advance the Reich. I wondered at how the use of the alien machinery could be justified under the laws of purity but I supposed they only applied to humans.

I waved the flatbeds through the portal much to the annoyance of the kommandant. His name flashed to the forefront of my mind as he strode angrily over to me from his armoured kubelwagen, demanding to know who had given me the authority to command his vehicles. Merkel was his name, and he paused in his tirade long enough to speak a command into his headset. The robots locked down into firing positions, their arm mounted cannon and machine guns scanning the courtyard for my unit. Even the Stürmgard would have trouble dealing with the twenty foot high combat automata.

I interrupted his puerile wittering. "Where is the Third Cohort?" I asked.

I did not listen to him as he expounded his views on the expendability and impurity of we Stürmgard half humans. I interfaced with the robots. I have no idea how I did this; it was as instinctive as breathing. The third cohort had been left to protect an area rich in alien technology several kilometres away, a task Merkel had received automatons for. A calculated insult. And he had left this Reichesfort with only a skeleton guard while he decided to have a jaunt through the wastelands surrounding us. The fool could have lost us the portal.

I over rode the automata's command codes and ordered them to patrol the perimeter of the fort. At the sound of them moving, Merkel turned in confusion and surprise and I shot him through the head, the three heavy bullets bursting his skull like an over ripe melon. The Reich has no need for incompetents like him. At the same time I felt a flash of guilt. Merkel was married and was father to four children. It was guilt I easily extinguished. If his children were lucky they would see him twice a year. And his wife would be little more than a brood mare destined to churn out little Hitler worshipping Nazis until her body gave out. She would be assigned another husband. Ja. There is little place for compassion in the Third Reich.

The presence of the Second Cohort ensured that my takeover of the Reichesfort command passed without incident. The Waffen SS were shocked at my summary execution of their kommandant; I could see it on their faces, but summary executions were not rare in the Reich. They would recover their composure quickly enough.

I knew what I had to do. I'm unsure where the orders came from, even now. Maybe they had been stored within my neo cortex implant to be released as the situation required, perhaps they were relayed to me via radio through the portal. I even considered the possibility that I was insane and I was hearing voices that I should not but I do not feel

I AM STEFAN STAHL

insane. I feel normal. Or as normal as an eight foot tall Stürmgard can be.

I wonder at what I am. I feel myself, I feel I am Stefan Stahl yet I most definitely am not. By that I mean this is not my body; my body was discarded and fed to the guard dogs of Schloss Schwabenstein. But I most definitely am **me**. I am superior though. An übermensch. If I want to know something I simply have to think about it and the information is there even though I know that I had no knowledge of it before my transformation. I can recall and recite each page, paragraph, sentence and word of Der Fuhrer's Mein Kampf. Before, I knew only the generalities and the sweeping vision it held within its pages. Disconcertingly I have this feeling, this nagging itch, that this revered script that is the bedrock of the Nazi state and all that is good about the Reich, is badly written nonsense. Even just writing this thought makes me feel ill though I do not eat anymore. I have no stomach, just a container to process solids into fuel. My fuel levels flash before my eyes, unconsciously brought up by my thoughts on nutrition; it is comforting to know that I have over a year left before I have to resupply.

I digress from my tale. An hour after my arrival on Neu Erde I decided to reconnoitre the surrounding area with an idea to establish forward observation posts to provide advance warning of any impending attack from the mutations that were present in the region. It was lonely on this dim alien planet. The Second Cohort did not speak and the Waffen SS were too afraid to approach me. They did the tasks allocated to them and kept themselves to themselves. As a soldier I could ask little more from them. As a man in everything but body, I felt an emptiness at the lack of human contact and missed the camaraderie between fellow men. The barren wilderness of the planet did not aid my mood. However, barren it may be, featureless it was not despite my initial brief impression. It was a bitterly cold place though I did not feel the cold pinch at me. My sensors indicated that the temperature was barely above zero degrees Celsius. The sun was a rare beast; a pale white disk at best , more often that not hidden by the thick grey clouds that spanned horizon to horizon, unspun by the constant wind that whined and wailed across the bare plains and round infrequent rocky outcrops. The land was the bland nothingness of depression, interspersed by far too rare streaks of pale pink and vibrant red.

On my initial reconnaissance, I examined the rocky outcrops closely as they would be ideal for observation posts being high with excellent lines of sight and having plenty of room for a small squad to base themselves comfortably. I was surprised to find the outcrops were all ruins of buildings, buildings that must have soared high into the sky, higher even that those of the Reich capital, Berlin. Their bottoms are lost beneath this desert sea but they go down, down, down, room after room after room, filled with dust, broken furniture and grinning skeletons. I wondered what had happened to this planet that had resulted in the decimation of such an advanced civilisation.

I established the outposts and allocated squads of Waffen SS to each one. The men seemed fearful, not a trait I would associate with the soldiers of such an organisation. I ignored their protests, putting it down to the general fear of the unknown.

When I was fourteen, a hospital truck visited the special hospice on the edge of town. The hospice was specifically for those who were retarded, either mentally or physically. The extensive grounds surrounding the whitewashed building were enclosed by a high brick wall which hid trees, lawns, colourful flowerbeds and, most importantly, the patients from the outside world. I remember idly thinking that it must have been a peaceful place to live save for the odd shriek, and occasional hoot of mad laughter.

I had a friend who was in the hospice, my best friend in fact. I remember Sebastian was good at climbing but my mother often warned me she considered him reckless. Sebastian had climbed one of the tallest trees in the nearby woods just to prove he could. When he was climbing down the tree, his foot had slipped, he lost his balance and he fell to the ground, hitting his head. Sebastian was never the same again. He could not look after himself from then on. He could not feed himself, clothe himself, do his toilet himself. Only a few months after the accident, his parents had put him in the hospice as they were unable to cope with his care and the shame.

I saw the line of patients dressed in hospital robes being gently herded into the back of the truck. I was shocked to see Sebastian gently swaying along, a big smile splitting his face. I nearly called out to him but then I remembered it wasn't Sebastian really. Not anymore. Then he saw me and a look of recognition passed across his face, his smile growing wider. He raised his hands and waved at me, and started towards me in a strange ambling ape like run, his loose hospital robes flapping as picked up speed. Luckily one of the hospital guards saw Sebastian break from the line and rushed over to divert my friend back towards the truck, leading him to the front of the queue where a white clad orderly helped Sebastian up the steps and into the truck. Once everyone was aboard the truck, the orderlies sealed the door with tape. While he did so, a masked man carefully opened a box and took out a round metal canister. I watched, fascinated, as he gingerly climbed a ladder placed at the side of the hospital truck and emptied the canister into a chimney. One of the orderlies passed cigarettes around while they chatted amicably to each other. I heard several thumps from inside the truck as if someone was trying to get out but the orderlies ignored them. Then it was quiet. The sun shone brightly down on this warm summer's day and the wind whispered in trees. Of course, I never saw Sebastian again.

The night of the first day descended quickly, the barely noticeable sun disappearing without suddenly, darkness simply appearing. The onyx night was almost complete broken only by the dazzling white spotlights of the robots which pounded unceasingly around the compound, the similarly harsh light from the guard towers at each corner of the Reichesfort and the distant splashes of yellow from the outposts. The wind continued its lonely lament for this dead world. On the horizon, thick ropes of blue and white lightning flashed and flared.

I did not sleep as I no longer had any need for rest. After I had debriefed the Waffen SS and collated data from the robots, I quickly formulated a plan to relieve the Stürmguard at Site Loki (which was the official designation of the archaeological dig) in the morning. The Second Cohort patrolled the walls to the relief of the exhausted SS. My initial desire was to join them in anticipation of a further attack from the mutations but something stopped me, a feeling, an instinct, a desire to uncover more about what I had become.

I needed to concentrate and so found myself a quiet room in the barracks block. The ceiling was far too low for me to stand, so settled down onto my legs, the motors and pistons complaining quietly as they locked into place. I closed my eyes, cutting myself off from the physical world and entered a vast metaphysical world of information. It was still and silent much like a library would be. I stretched my senses and detected the robots, the dumb automatons following their predefined patrol patterns without pause or boredom. They have no sensors of any kind save for a few rudimentary light sensors that are limited to detecting light in the human visible spectrum. That was the best our scientists could do with the technology that is so beyond comprehension that it makes our own efforts seem like a stick of wood.

I left the robots to follow their program, and brought my attention inwards to explore the library, the information appearing simply by my thinking of a subject. Such as Castle Schwabenstein. The schloss had been home to an SS garrison before the beginning of the war, a garrison of which a significant number of the soldiers were under the thrall of the Thule Cult. An accident had occurred which had left the entire garrison dead. The Ahnenerbe claimed an uncontrollable physical manifestation of Thule himself had caused the accident but how they knew this was not explained probably because it was nonsense. The physical manifestation of a god? Someone had spent too much time reading Grimm's fairy tales. Whatever had occurred had left its mark on the skin of the universe. When the portal between Germany and Hyde Park in London had been opened, a rip had appeared in the underground chamber that had been stabilised by the incumbent at the time, SS-Gruppenführer Doktor Jaegerstass of SS Secret Project Division Deimos. This dim world is what lay through the rip. The few brief explorations had uncovered vast amounts of alien technology but it was so difficult to understand and make practical use of that only the robots and Stürmgard had come out of the research. This was the reason that Der Fuhrer had stalled the war with Britain for so long - he had understood that the potential of the alien technology was enormous and the possibilities had been barely touched. Why waste German lives fighting an enemy on equal terms when one could crush them beneath the jackboot of invincible technological might?

The Stürmgard is the result of alien technology? This fact jolted me out of my stasis. Not only was I not completely human but I was alien too. How could I say that I am pure Aryan now? My blood and body are befouled and tainted. But I did not feel different. I am still Stefan Stahl. My feelings, my thoughts and my beliefs are mine even if I was wrapped up in this metal body. How others perceived me was of no importance. I am Stefan Stahl.

Yet even as I write this I know that others will not, DO not, see it this way - I am not human anymore in appearance so how can I be of Aryan blood? People are always afraid of that which is different, be it Jews, Negros or übermensch.

A flashing dot drew my attention to the chronograph on the edge of my vision. I hooked into the robots' sensors to see that the sun was apparently above the horizon and that I had been meditating for several hours. I say apparently as the only indication of the dawn was the pale light flooding across the desolate grey plains. The mission to Site Loki was due to set off in four minutes. As I thought about the mission, a map appeared in front of me, indicating the location of the Second Cohort. They were already moving into a loose delta formation at the gate in readiness for me to lead them. I decided to leave the robots behind. Compared to the Stürmgard they were too slow and the weakened Waffen SS garrison required their support. Reinforcements were on course to be sent through the portal soon enough but I was not in the mood to take risks. The planet unsettled me for an indefinable reason. I didn't wish to stay there any longer than I had to. If the mutations captured the fort and the enclosed portal, I would have been furious.

The wind had risen in the past few hours, still whistling from the North, still bitter. I felt it pinch my exposed face as I stepped out into the quadrangle before I lowered my visor. I could see the SS guards shivering as they watched me lead my cohort out the still broken gate, presumably from the chill. I wondered briefly if the SS here were a punishment detail but dismissed the thought when I noticed they were wearing winter clothing.

I projected a map containing waypoints and strategical details out to the cohort and sent them on their way. I had forgotten some things in my haste to depart.

I called to Obersturmführer Bannhoff who was supervising the construction of a new gate. I noted with approval that it was a far sturdier construction than the one which had stood before it.

I startled the man, much as I startled myself. My voice creaked out with difficulty from a disused throat. I heard it rattle and wheeze within the confines of my visor. What Bannhoff heard was a blaring mechanical monotone. It had an immediate effect as he ran over to me and saluted smartly.

"You are in command until my return," I heard myself croak quietly with its brass blare in parallel. He nodded but stayed mute as he craned his neck to look up at me waiting to be dismissed. I was about to do so when his mouth half opened before closing.

"You have a question?" I asked, both of us wincing at the grating voice.

Bannhoff was a young man (so am I! Or should I say 'was'?) and appeared to be overcome by my presence yet he pulled himself together and asked. "Sir, I do not have many men to defend the Reichesfort and I have been notified that it will be a day before we receive reinforcements. We have several reconnaissance units of Tyrannosaurkavallerie exploring nearby. Do you have any idea when they will return?"

I was about to respond in the negative when Bannhoff disappeared from my sight to be replaced by a satellite image of the surrounding region, 50 kilometres square. The detail was incredible and I was easily able to pick out the four Tyrannosaurkavallerie units, each one consisting of three riders. All were loping homewards and making good speed. Bannhoff was relieved to hear this, though he seemed as puzzled as I was as to how I knew so precisely the location of each unit. I suspect that this unyielding body that I inhabit has many surprises, few of which I am consciously aware of, and I am fairly certain that even the General Doktor does not know the full extent of my capabilities. I did not know what I a satellite was then my mind reeled as it attempted to assimilate and process the new and fantastic knowledge that had some how been injected in to it.

I caught up easily with the Second Cohort and settled at the forefront of the delta formation at an easy run. Our bodies do not tire, we do not rest. There is a road of sorts that we follow. The ground was crushed and compacted beneath the weight of half tracks and lorries passing back and forth many times. Hills rose on either side of us, some rolling, some tall and vertical with soaring cliffs.

#The remnants of a once great city#

A voice spoke from just behind my right shoulder, startling me. I span round but only the Second Cohort was behind me, none near enough to have said anything to me. They sped onwards, ignoring me as

I fruitlessly scanned the cliffs for signs of life. My internal chronometer showed that I am missing twenty two seconds. What happened in those missing seconds? Was I turned off somehow? I did not know the answers nor did I believe that I was turned off. I am not an automation. A systems check confirmed that my existing systems were fully functional and had been since my rebirth two weeks perviously. My mood was greatly disturbed and gravely unsettled but I continued my journey nonetheless, burying my worries beneath the weight of duty.

The road was long with many diversions from the direct route but we made good time and it was just before noon that I led the Second Cohort in to a wide open space at the far end of which was a cliff face pockmarked with cave openings - Site Loki. The First Cohort were well hidden but I knew where to look, finding all nine before we were halfway across the square. I beamed out an identifier signal and they stood down though they were still wary - they had detected large movements of mutations overnight, movements far larger than any that had been detected or seen previously.

It dawns on me then that I have been very much in command, not just of my cohort but of all the German forces. I could understand the Waffen SS accepting my orders as I was after all a Stürmgard, but the First Cohort accepted my order to stand down with no complaint even from Kohl, their squad leader. It puzzled me.

#It is because you are an Oberst-Grupenführer. Your orders override all others. Who are you? Your DNA shows impurities. How are you implanted in a Blitzsoldat?#

The voice spoke again. My chronograph showed a further black out period of fifty eight seconds. I did not understand what was happening to me. My head, no... my brain itched abominably as if ants were matching across it, every step they took scratching and tickling; irritating.

Site Loki irritated me for an indefinable reason. It was a complex that had survived the disaster that had consumed this alien planet.

Long wide corridors split the buried building into large open plan rooms filled with long dead equipment covered in the dust of ages. Although I had intended to return to the Reichesfort immediately with the First Cohort, I could not contain my curiosity and explored the mausoleum further. Occasionally I entered a room and was assailed by a montage of images superimposed over the grey ruins, images which I am sure showed the original appearance of the room. Masked shadowy figures glided across my vision. Robotic arms twisted and manipulated where now they hung limp and corroded above dead machinery that silently displayed images and calculations in holographic hard light in my visions. I should have recognised this place. Recognised each every room. I had been there before! I knew I had!

I wondered at the sanctity of this metal suit I inhabited. Blood and steel, the purity of a warrior. I poked and prodded it experimentally. I had looked upon this body without seeing. There must be more to it than this impregnable skin, I thought. What lay beneath? Motors, artificial treble bound silicon fibre muscle, a hydrogen powered engine, state of the art tactical computation cores, a Hochmeister class intelligence, holographic display interfaces - data suddenly started to scroll across my vision, bewildering in its intensity, images of each component flashing by and zooming in at a sickening pace. My head span with the information overload and I felt myself reeling back trying to escape from the deluge of data. It shames me to admit that I screamed, such was my fearful state of mind.

I must have blacked out due to the overwhelming injection of data. I slowly came to and was puzzled and alarmed to find myself stumbling along a corridor towards an archway of significant height which enclosed a set of closed double doors. They were intimidating in both their height and apparent solidity. I had little doubt that not even a Tiger tank would have been able to break through them. As I regained motor control, I looked behind me to see a ragged line of footprints scuffed into the thick dust of the floor disappearing in to the unlit distance. As I looked, a spark of light flashed on far away, obscured by the still settling dust.

The twin doors blocked the way ahead of this solid and impermeable cul de sac. The air felt heavy; heavy with the weight of age and expectation. The lights set into the plain ceiling above hummed and yellow light welled across the doors, highlighting flecks of red and a weave of deep scratch marks across the centre of the two door.

I sensed the mutations before I heard their long sonorous howls echoing down the long corridor towards me. I felt the red mist descending, my heart beat faster and my muscles swelled as drugs and chemicals were automatically fed into my artificial body. With a mental command, I turned them off. I valued the clear head of a soldier of the SS, not the thoughtless rage of a beast. I heard a murmur of approval from next to me but when I whirled round to see who had spoken, I was faced only by a grey wall.

I was without cover but I did not think I would need any. The mutations I had destroyed at the Reichesfort were armed only with the claws and horns that erupted from their twisted bodies. I felt the heft of my triple barrelled MG47, patting it like it was a pet. The unfortunate mutations would be cut down long before they reached me, an inconvenience at worst.

The beast was enormous, easily filling the corridor as it skidded around the distant corner and galloped towards me with its head down, mismatched plates of multicoloured armour exposing only weeping red eyes. Elongated tusks curved forwards to meet in front of its head all covered in elaborate decorations visible across the rapidly closing distance.

My writing is a barely legible scrawl that covers page after page after page. It feels that I am merely transcribing a recording of my thoughts. I think that everything that I have seen, heard, even smelt is recorded somewhere in my head and that there is no need to keep this diary as I have perfect recall. Yet I feel compelled to continue writing. It is a compulsion I cannot ignore, like an addiction or a craving to inscribe my thoughts and recollection in written format. I am struggling to separate the present time from the past that I am committing to paper. I continue writing, the sight of the diminutive pen gliding across the paper fading away as I once again immerse myself in the events of just a few days ago.

A hunchbacked humanoid sat on the back of the beast with its hands on control rods, a shout of delight escaping its lopsided mouth as it extorted its charge recklessly on. A targeting reticle formed over the rider as I took aim, the distance counting down with a terrifying rapidity. Eighty metres, sixty, forty, twenty... My gun bucked as I fired, the heavy calibre bullets almost instantly turning the mutant rider into a lumpen skrag end of flesh. A fraction of a second later, I leapt high into the air, the thundering beast passing below me as my back scraped the ceiling of the corridor.

#Targets: 32. Unarmed. Human. DNA corrupted by tachyon radiation exposure. Unrecoverable. Impure. Execute#

As landed amidst the mutations, from behind me I heard bone splinter and a wet thud as swollen flesh met immutable concrete. The things determined to kill me looked aghast as I reared above them. Then I killed them. My gun growled and spat flame as brass cases clattered to the floor. Skin split and cratered, tainted blood sprayed in elegant fans drawn out by the supersonic bullets; limbs exploded as they were ineffectually drawn across terrified eyes, bone splintered, wounds gaped. Curved blades sprang out from the back of my left gauntlet, glinting with a greasy silver sheen in the yellow light. As I swept my gun round in a fiery arc to my right, so I mirrored that arc with my left hand, barely feeling skin and bone part in gouts of blood, barely hearing the screams of pain, the slop of internal organs as they unravelled like great purple worms, and the splatter of liquid against the walls.

Seconds had passed. Seconds. A limb, a body spasmed in its death throes. The stench of cordite and voided bowels filled my nostrils. Where my sensors detected a body (which was not an easy task given the state the dead were in) a flat line showed them devoid of life. Nothing lived save for one, an uneven irregular pulse disrupting the straight line of death. With morbid curiosity, I crouched next to the mutilated being. What sort of thing was this alien...

#Human#

...human? Reaching out carefully, I removed the rounded helmet that covered the person's face, noticing a sharp spike in the ragged heartbeat as I did so. Despite the warped and twisted body, the face was undoubtedly human, a chance of fate lending it the beautiful symmetry of the ancient sculptures I once saw in the Vatican. Blue eyes clouded with pain were partly hidden by strands of straw blonde hair. The girl (of this I had no doubt) struggled to speak, unable to form her words as blood frothed and bubbled form her mouth. I had nothing to wipe it away with nor did I trust my clumsy fingers to do so. A thought flashed through my mind - why should I do so? Why care for the last moments of an obviously unclean abomination?

#Because it is the right thing to do. Because it is... human#

Words burbled out. Much to my astonishment they were in German, though in a dialect I was not familiar with. Nonetheless it was perfectly understandable.

"This is your fault," she said. "You reaped what you sowed."

Then her eyes rolled back into her head, exposing only the whites, and a final pained gasp spluttered from between her lips as he fell back to lie in the morass of blood, shit and body parts.

Her words did not register with me at first, such was my shock at not just seeing a human face but hearing German spoken.

My fault? How was it my fault? Too many questions I did not have answers to. Too many questions I barely understood.

A pained grunt drew my attention towards the bloodied hulk that had been guided on a suicide run into the great doors. Hooves scrabbled for purchase, eliciting high pitched squeals as they failed to find any. I strode up to the animal and fired a burst of shots into its head through a gap in its armour. A beast it may be but it did not need to suffer.

The Jews suffered. My friends and I used to go looking for Jews to torment. They were easy to find at first as the yellow stars they wore on their jackets singled them out like a black sheep in a flock of white. Men, women, children. It made no difference.

"You're next!" We shouted, referring to the eviction and resettlement programme. "Auf wiedersehen!"

"Better practice working!" was a favourite of my friend, Sebastian. As everyone knew, all Juden are lazy.

Sometimes we could not be bothered shouting and just threw stones at them much as we would at the stray dogs.

But as the months passed it became too much effort to find Jews to make fun of and abuse as they were all eventually rounded up and sent to the work camps.

#Extermination camps#

That voice again. Should I ignore it, I wondered to myself.

#You can ignore me if you wish. I will be still be here#

Tentatively, unwilling to acknowledge my madness, I asked, "Who are you?"

#Finally! It asks the sensible question! I am the Hochmeister intelligence encased within the Blitzsoldat armour you wear#

I chose to ignore the voice. I would not give in to the creeping madness. I felt a tickle of frustration that I was unsure was my own.

I spied a gap where the seemingly impregnable doors had been damaged by the rampaging leviathan. The gap leading to the beyond was small, barely large enough for me to squeeze through. I was forced to hack away bloody chunks of shattered skull, leaving the brain to fall out to the floor in a large gelatinous mass. Once I had completed my gory task I was able to slide through the gap between the two doors.

#Brace yourself#

I could not believe my eyes. My face visor rose silently to allow me an unobstructed view of the incredible chamber I suddenly found myself in, the vastness of which I struggle to describe. Lights shone from the ceiling far above, soft and strong like summer sunshine, illuminating a long shallow slope before me that ended near the centre of this kilometre long hall designed for giants, just as another slope started its ascent to the far end. On either side of the twin slopes ran parallel roads, alongside which stood rows upon rows of gleaming figures, details of which I was unable to discern due to the height at which I stood. All those details I noticed only later as I had fallen to my knees as I staggered under the combined weight of confusion and terror. I blinked rapidly, trying to erase the insane and unbelievable image from sight, unable and, I have no doubt now, unwilling to accept the reality of what was in front of me.

On the far side of the hall, directly opposite me and barely visible in the distance, lay what appeared to be a sarcophagus bathed in a pure cleansing light. Behind the sarcophagus rose a carving of an Imperial German eagle, so large that its wings spanned the entire rear wall. I know it was an Imperial German eagle as it clutched an equally giant swastika in its claws. On either side stood figures of such a scale that I did not recognise them at first for what they were. Planted at ground level, the statues soared high until they stood above even the sarcophagus and its protective eagle; two SS stormtroopers, their faces grim, right arms outstretched in a familiar salute.

I reeled. There is no other word for it. I felt as if my skull was being constantly pounded by a hammer. If I could have gasped for breath, I would have gasped. So, ja, I reeled, my vision spinning, and it was then that all doubt was erased as to the validity of what I was seeing, as I saw for the first time, the two rows of giant stormtroopers on either side of the hall, all saluting.

#I warned you. Perhaps next time you will listen to me. I am applying a small cocktail of chemicals to your system to calm you down. A mild sedative, nothing more.#

Even as I formed a protest, I felt my hysteria melt away and I was able to see clearly, both visually and mentally. It was time I had a conversation with myself.

#Not with yourself you dumbkopf. With me!#

I ignored the insult. "Who are you? What are you?"

#There is no need to speak. I am a part of you now. Your thoughts are my thoughts. To answer your question, I repeat what I told you earlier. I am a Hochmeister artificial machine intelligence. You are in an Odin class Blitzsoldat armoured suit though I do not understand how a fool such as yourself could find himself elevated to such a level. Standards must be slipping.#

I am a Sturmgard, I protested silently.

#Blitzsoldat, Stürmgard, they are the same. If it makes you happier then I will say you are Stürmgard.#

The voice was tetchy with a vaguely familiar accent. Almost... British.

#Ja, ja. I was born in Britain.#

'Born'? 'Britain'?

#Good grief son. Are you a man or a parrot?#

Neither, I said. I am most definitely not your 'son' and I don't believe I am a man anymore at all.

#Hah. That was just a figure of speech. Perhaps you are not as stupid as I feared. That is a most perceptive observation, one that many of those transplanted into Blitzsoldat armour apparently struggle with. Nein, you are not a man anymore. You have ascended the constraints of flesh and blood and all the impurities imbued in you by Mother Nature. Congratulations.#

The computer...

#Machine intelligence!#

...Was being sarcastic.

#Just a little bit. But enough! The burning question is 'Where am I'? Am I right?#

Ja...

#A rhetorical question. Now silence yourself and I will answer. This is the mausoleum of the great First Fuhrer of the Thousand Year Reich, Adolf Hitler, who died in the 58th Year of the Reich. God rot his black, evil, damned soul.#

This is Earth? I expected a sharp rebuttal. Of course it was Earth. How else could I be seeing what I was seeing? But how?

#Yes, this is Earth although it is far into your future. I have communicated with various satellites that are still operational and they say that this is 139YR.#

139YR?

#2072 by your reckoning. Give it a few years in your own time and you'll soon start using the proper date notation.#

This is the future then, I thought to myself, surprised at how calmly I accepted this information. The drugs must have still been coursing around my nervous system. What happened to Earth?

#The time gate exploded. It was kept open for many, many years as this time was plundered of technology. The Reich achieved its aim of world domination as no one, including Britain, could stand against the advanced technology of this future.#

Realisation suddenly dawned upon me. General Doktor Jaegerstass doesn't know this! He thinks this is an alien planet!

#More than likely. Now do you want me to continue or have you somehow magically guessed the entire story? I thought so. Now hush. I'm telling you the brief version. Your Reich scientists were an arrogant bunch and ignored the blindingly obvious signs that the gate was unstable. Massive fluctuations in the gate's power consumption, earthquakes in what was a geologically stable part of the world, time distortions in the areas around Castle Schwabenstein, people and equipment being lost in the journey between the two portals, spatial warping over areas so large that it was visible from space, the list goes on and on. Then one day, kaboom! No one knows exactly what happened except perhaps those standing next to the portal when it did its nuclear explosion impression. The crater is five hundred kilometres south of here.#

A map flashed in front of me on which I could see a barren circular depression that dwarfed the nearby city of Munich. Or what remained of Munich I should say, as it was obvious from the intricate detail that it was all but ruins.

#It was an extinction level event. Dust filled the Earth's atmosphere, temperatures plummeted and radiation spilled out from the site. No crops or plants grew. Those that did froze. All the animals died off except a few hardy insects. Then all the people starved. Against the odds, a few survived, their descendants becoming the mutations you've already met. The end. And here we are now.#

Earth! The Reich! All gone!

#The Reich likely survives somewhere, as I have no doubt that a few of the elite arranged for their own escape to either one of the Moon or Mars bases. It has always been the case that the privileged few escape unscathed from the problems they have caused, leaving the proletariat behind to suffer.#

I can stop this from happening. If I tell General Doktor Jaegerstass what I have seen and learned then he will surely shut down the time portal.

#Good luck with that my little munchkin. Your General Doktor will not risk having his meteoric rise through the Nazi hierarchy stymied by a lone foot soldier such as you. And you are nothing in the eyes of the Nazi war machine, nothing. A fancy robot to be sacrificed in place of those deemed to be of good Germanic stock. Don't make me laugh. And I hate to say it but it's already happened - the gate exploded years ago now.#

A strange feeling came over me then. A determination that I would prevent the destruction of the Reich at all costs compounded by a wave of despair - could I change the course of time? Was such a thing possible?

Will you help me?

#Why should I help you prevent the downfall of the most murderous, bigoted and downright disgusting regime that the world has known? Hmmm?#

I knew the answer straight away. Because billions will die if you don't.

As I turned to leave, a flash of light caught my eye. I bent down and found what appeared to be a silver swastika on the floor almost entirely covered in dust save for a single edge that was perhaps uncovered by a draught when the door opened. I am not sentimental but it reminded me of the silver swastikas that my parents hung from the fir tree during the Winter Solstice. I picked it up and placed it in a compartment of my armour.

The Wounded Titan

From this point onwards my recollection of the events on Neu Erde are not recorded in my journal though I can replay them in my mind's eye with a clarity and lucidity that I find intimidating. I am uncertain as to why I do not write down this part of my journey and as to why I feel the need for secrecy.

I walked back to the complex's entrance as if someone was holding me by the hand. The interior was as vast as the mausoleum suggested, and it took me some time to traverse the many miles of corridor. I did wonder what lay behind the frequent double doors spaced at regimentally regular intervals but I was still processing the shocking discovery of just a few minutes previously; I did not care enough to investigate.

As I reached the upper levels of the complex, my radio communications hummed and crackled back into life and I was assaulted by a deluge of calm emotionless requests for orders. In the background I heard a long drawn out groan as if a titan from legends long since past was awakening. My metaphor proved to be unfortunately accurate as I discovered when stepped out of the entrance vestibule.

#Oh good grief and bloody hell. A Death's Head battle robot.#

A robot? Can I interface with it and tell it to stand down?

#Not a chance. It has hardened communication channels only accessible by the High Command. Totally outside your sphere of influence I'm afraid. We're in trouble.#

But it's just a robot. Uhhh... I looked up and up and up. And then even further up.

The Death's Head towered over the surrounding walls by tens of meters, sand and dust still pouring from its rounded carapace, down its V shaped torso and then over its trio of legs. Joints creaked and groaned as it straightened up, a massive metal monument to destruction that blocked the pale disc of the sun. A steel god of annihilation. Why three legs...?

#A more stable gun platform. Talking of which...#

The aforementioned weapons were attached to the end of thick arms which in turn appeared from opposing sides of the machine's torso. A shining silver skull grinned at us from under a rounded carapace, its red eyes blazing as it scanned we insects that had violated Der Fuhrer's eternal sleep.

Long disused gears ground and crunched as a gatling cannon the size of five Tiger tanks was activated and pointed our way. I could quite easily have crawled into one of the barrels with room to spare. I could hear the ammunition belts clanking as they fed massive shells into the gun from the machine's hoppers.

#Hit the deck! Get down! NOW!#

I didn't hesitate, relaying the order to the two cohorts of Stürmgard as I threw myself to the ground. A fraction of a second later and my audio filters kicked in as the cannon screamed and the world exploded around me.

Why is it firing on us? Surely it can identify the Stürmgard armour as friendly?

#God only knows. Could be that it's feeling cranky and needs to blow off some steam.#

What?

A swathe of wall above me disintegrated as an uncountable number of cannon shells slammed into it, the explosions like firecrackers to my filtered hearing, the buffeting from the shockwaves proving they were anything but.

#I don't know! Stop asking me ridiculous questions and stop that thing before it kills us all!#

The storm of fire stopped as a grating clunk signalled a jam on the undoubtedly rusty firing mechanism. I hoped and was rewarded by a torrent of sparks that was swiftly followed by a dirty explosion of deep onyx black striped by yellow and red that ripped the massive cannon from its mounting. A building that was too close to the machine collapsed in a beige pillar of dust.

How do I stop this machine?

#I've pulled up the schematics. It's bullet proof, bomb proof, laser proof, everything proof. Unless you've got a nuclear weapon lying about then we're mincemeat.#

I didn't know what a laser or a nuclear weapon were but I let it pass. My mind raced. It was a robot. Therefore it had a power source to run it, a brain to think.

#That's right. But they're inside the...#

I jumped to my feet, ordering the two cohorts forward with me, noting their cool blue identifying signals on my internal screen. Two were missing. A loss was a loss but only two was a small loss. I spared a look back and almost stopped. The Death's Head had fired only for three seconds but Site Loki had practically disappeared. It was nothing short of a miracle that anyone was still alive!

Scale the machine, I ordered. Find a way inside it and destroy everything you see. Stop it at any cost!

#No! Death's Heads are armed with anti personal...#

Even the voice at my shoulder was drowned out as machine guns opened fire from their turrets underslung beneath the giant's torso. The Stürmgard armour provided excellent protection but even it failed under the hail of shells. Braun and Beckenbaur were sprinting hard towards the towering leg nearest to them when twin trails of gunfire fixed on them, blowing them backwards off their feet. Sparks and wires slopped out from broken arms and amputated legs. A line of smoking and blackened craters crossed Braun's chest leading up to his helmet which was now a mangled ruin. I was surprised to see Beckenbaur sit up despite missing a leg and an arm and attempt to stand. A savage barrage of gunfire threw Beckenbaur back down, his limbs flailing as the shells exploded through his chest. He didn't get up again. Two blue dots disappeared from my display. My men were being slaughtered.

Away to my left I saw three Stürmgard cut down, the ground exploding around them as they futilely attempted to dodge the implacable machine eyes of the Death's Head. Three more lights gone.

I sprinted towards the four toed leg in front of me. It was the only course of action I could take. The shadow of the colossus fell across me, streams of thin sunlight through the girders that crisscrossed to form the massive legs. I weaved as gunshots exploded around me, shrapnel and stones pinging and clattering into me from all directions. More blue spots disappeared from the display. And then I was staring up at this massive foot where each toe was riveted slabs of rusted metal, each as tall as I was. The rivets made for an easy climb and I quickly reached the attached leg and its crosswork of riveted girders and uncovered motors. I almost fell off as the foot suddenly lifted from the ground, the toes dipping in a way that reminded me of an ostrich or emu that I once saw at Berlin zoo. I felt the grinding of motors and the clunk clunk of an unhealthy engine as I held on to a girder. The wounded death machine was turning. Something had caught its attention.

#There's a mutation encampment nearby. The Death's Head has likely spotted it.#

From overhead came a deep buzz barely on the edge of even my enhanced hearing followed by a shower of sparks and crackles of electric lightning. Polarising filters flicked down over my eyes even before the deep whoomph that nearly shook me from my perch.

#That was a plasma cannon. I wouldn't like to be on the other end of that. Hurry up and break this thing!#

I swiftly scaled to the top of the limb, keeping on the outside so the machine guns could not fire on me, to be faced with a wall of tubing, plates, wiring and metal structure.

#We've been lucky. It appears that this is an unfinished Death's Head as it's missing its armour. Lucky for us. The power generator will be somewhere in the midst of that mess.#

What about the brain?

#Ditto. Though higher up.#

I unsheathed my blade, drew it back. As I pulled my arm back, the weak sun glinted off a something moving. A gun! I swung round to flatten myself against a support just as the gun blazed and hot lead whined past my head. The gun clicked on its cupola as it tried to adjust its angle of fire. Without waiting to sigh with relief, I swung round again, hurling myself upwards towards the gun that was still jerking on its mount. I slashed down with my blade, slicing through the gun barrel with ease as I caught hold of the cupola and crashed round into the exposed mass of cables. I had no idea what I was doing but I slashed through everything I could see, pulled and tore cables and conduits from their sockets, slashed and tore, slashed and tore.

#Calm down. You've done the job. Well done.#

The Death's Head stood still and silent, the wind whining through the forest of cables.

#That's only the second time a Death's Head has been stopped in its tracks. We were lucky it wasn't armoured nor fully operational otherwise we'd be dead and scrap metal.#

Just like this machine now is.

I pushed my way out through the tangles and took a moment to take in the view from on high. In the near distance, a mushroom cloud billowed into the sky, its peak already torn by the winds. Beneath it, broken buildings stood like rotten teeth around a glass crater of ever increasing circles. Small figures scuttled away, some blazing like candles. To my left the shattered frontage of the mausoleum complex could not even be said to stand such had been the destruction from the Death's Head cannon fire. However, the building was so massive that only a small percentage had been destroyed. Much of it must be underground as I could easily see over the roof to cathedral like domes and sky scraping spires beyond that had somehow survived the devastation that had racked this world. To my right was the road to the Reichesfort winding round the tops of buried buildings and what would now be barrow mounds full of the dead. This whole world, this Neu Erde was a mausoleum, a monument to a dead race survived by beings that are an anathema to the principles of National Socialism and racial purity. A relic of failure. I must ensure that this future Erde does not happen.

#But you're happy to forward the ideal of National Socialism and racial purity. Tsk. Use your brain boy. There can be no future for either. A dictatorship where power rests in the hands of the few, and trust me when I say you're not one of the few no matter what you're told, and a founding principle that cannot ever be met as the truth of racial intermixing is exposed as technology becomes more and more advanced.#

I ignored the sniping and a resolve formed within my heart... #You don't have a heart.#... resolve formed within my heart to close the time portal.

With a look down, I jumped from girder to girder of the deathly still titan before landing at its foot next to two of the first cohort who were in guard position, automatically scanning for targets or anything out of place. I quickly checked my viewer and was relieved to discover most of the Second Cohort still lived, if they could be said to live, with only three of my kameraden cut down by the Death's Head's weapons. The senior cohort had proved to be less lucky, a fact I could see with my own eyes. Seven of the nine First Cohort Stürmgard lay across the courtyard in pieces, limbs twitching whether they were still attached to their armoured torsos or not, clear fluid dripping from tubes in to puddles of blood like oil. I directed the remaining Stürmgard to form a secure perimeter around us while I took the opportunity to examine a dead Stürmgard. I had no idea what I looked like inside this armour. I had an itch to know.

Of the ten dead Stürmgard, eight had been shot repeatedly in the chest area where the heavy shellfire had eviscerated the soldiers, reducing whatever lay within to smoking ruin. Two of the Stürmgard lay decapitated, one by a shot to the neck which had ripped its head off and sent it sailing away, the other from a shot that had exploded its head in a shower of shrapnel and brain matter. Stürmgard armour was not meant to be unsealed once closed yet I knew instinctively where the hidden joins were and slowly applied increasing pressure to them until they popped. The breastplate came away easily. I was intrigued to find that the armour was not metal as I had always presumed but that it was an incredibly light material made of interlocking strands of black and silver.

#It's carbon-titanium fibre. Cutting edge 21st century armour.#

I grunted as I placed the armour plate aside. The terms meant nothing to me though I could feel the information trickling into my mind to be recalled if I required. I peered with interest into the chest cavity of the deceased man-machine. There was even less flesh and blood than I had expected, with thick bundles of wiring and tubing taking the place of muscles and sinew. As I examined the intricate network of equipment, data flashed up in front of me, boxes and circles highlighting each device within. The power supply sat where the stomach would be, a cylinder that glowed slightly from within, which had many power conduits snaking out and connecting to the various motor systems around the armour. Then there was the power regulator, a sphere of ridged grey plastic; a large black box sat alone with unconnected wiring ports, which was where the machine intelligence lived in the case of Blitzsoldat commanders; a small computational device, balance regulation system and fire control aid were plugged into a plastic board next to the black box while to the left of the power supply was the solid fuel and pharmaceutical creation system, a variety of connected cylinders and spheres from which a wide tube led up to where the head was once attached and various smaller tubes led to the power supply and to the only human part of the machine - the spine. Obviously there had been a brain as well but it was currently spread out over the courtyard. The spine had been suspended in a clear cylinder filled with the fluid that was now sinking into the thirsty dust.

#You could just have asked me for a schematic you know# my conscience chided.

I wanted to see for myself what made me a Stürmgard. So little of me remains.

#Of your physical body, yes. It has been argued that your body is just a puppet of meat controlled by your brain. Now you are in a puppet of metal and plastic but you are still in control.#

I shook my head. I could see the logic but it ran counter to my indoctrination that Aryan blood runs pure. What am I if I have no blood?

#'Indoctrination'. You said it, not me. Any knowledge you learn through indoctrination will always be suspect.#

I stood up, staring at the naked Stürmgard, quite unable to tear my eyes away from its lack of humanity. It was a machine, a robot, a mindless drone much like the Deaths Head sentinel. A thought struck me.

Is the Deaths Head a larger version of the Blitzsoldat?

#I couldn't say. The files are classified even to me. I do have the same suspicions as you. The reason human brains are used is that they are incredible powerful computational devices capable of processing and analysing multiple streams of data and acting on them immediately. Even in the future, a machine intelligence is unable to match a natural brain.#

What are you then? I asked genuinely puzzled.

#I am a human intelligence imprinted into a machine intelligence core. There's nothing artificial about my intelligence!#

I gazed up at the Deaths Head, finally able to take in the massiveness of the machine and the destructive power it wielded. If it fell into the hands of the Third Reich, conquering the world of 1943 would become inevitable. Nations would surrender at even the threat of this titan of destruction treading on their lands. So why do I dread such a happening?

#Because you're not stupid, SS poster boy. You've not been completely brainwashed. Deep down you know that the Reich and its leaders are, quite simply, wrong.#

Blood, Power, Stupidity

I open my eyes, hopeful, praying even, that I have experienced a dream. An extremely vivid dream but a dream nonetheless. My hopes are dashed as my eye is drawn to the small swastika of silver that peeks out from beneath the mound of paper sitting on my desk.

#The journal is now unnecessary. I subtly encouraged you to recall your experiences on Neu Erde, as you so quaintly call it, to aid your neurological systems adaption to the Blitzsoldat unit, its systems and my own machine intelligence. We are not quite as one but we are close enough.#

You will always be in my head? Always? The thought was not appealing.

#Always.# The voice was firm. #However, if you tell me to shut up then I will. At the same time I will not hesitate to interfere if you are about to bugger things up.#

Talking of which. I must present my findings to General Doktor Jaegerstass. He will know what to do. I must stop Erde being destroyed.

#Your findings? What findings? You have no evidence to present to the General Doktor. He will laugh in your face before dissecting you to find out how you work. You will kill both of us.#

But what can I do? I do not wish to see the Reich turned into a barren wasteland simply because I did not speak out.

#Huh. Yet you will happily see entire villages, towns and peoples razed and murdered in the name of racial purity.#

I was taken aback by the vehemence of the statement. How can I have a voice inside me that does not agree with Nazi ideals? Our superior Nazi scientists could not allow such a thing, surely?

#Your 'superior' Nazi scientists messed up when they made me. I was likely a rush job or a Friday-night-before-beers muck up but whatever the reason, your 'superior' Nazi scientists forgot to run the Indoctrination Protocol. I am still me, unfettered by the stupidity of

Nazi Racial Purity propaganda and all the idiocy that resulted from that.#

But racial purity is necessary for the continuation of the German race. And we need and deserve the living space!

#Yes, yes. What a load of manure.# There was a rustle of static, like a sigh. #You are just a boy, still. You have had no chance to think for yourself, always bombarded by Nazi Party lies. Let me ask you something - what are the Jews?#

The Jews are an unclean race that financially exploited decent Germans and ground us all down to poverty.

#Said like a true SS poster boy. Do you think the Jews all deserved to die?#

They are unclean. Their blood is full of impurities.

#Is that right? And what about an average German. How pure are they?#

This discussion was rapidly ascending to a level I was unable to respond to. Nonetheless I tried. The Board for Racial Purity traces peoples descendants back generations. Any Jews in their bloodline are identified and judgement is passed.

#That's the way it is now. In the future, where I come from, there is something called DNA testing.# Images and data flooded my mind, feeding and educating me as they were injected directly into my cerebral cortex. All of a sudden I was an expert on the topic of DNA. My head hurt. #DNA testing allows 'impurities' to found in everyone from your so called untermensch all the way up to the blonde blue eyed Nordics you Nazis are so fond of.#

I tidied the stack of paper as I worked my way through the data I had been fed. A scientific paper appeared, the conclusive sentence from its obvious bulk detaching and hovering in front of it 'The only way to ensure blood and flesh purity is to remove it from the purity equation.'

#In other words, you create machines of steel and chrome and add a German brain. But if the impurities of flesh and blood and skin colour can be removed then surely the Jews can be liberated from their taints?#

Philosophical discussions were never my strong point.

#That's probably why you joined the SS. The point I was trying to make was that if you believe you have conquered the impurities of the body then you must turn your attention to impurities of thought. If thought can be restricted then you create slaves. At what point does your superhuman Aryan race turn into slaves?#

Like me?

Static crackled. #No, not like you. You have your freedom to think what you wish. Your compatriots of the First and Second Cohorts are not so lucky. You were installed in a kommandant Blitzsoldat so you already had more freedom of thought. Plus you have me and I did not apply any barriers or restrictions to your thoughts.#

I shuffle the last pieces of my journal together before passing an electric current through the wedge of paper to set it on fire before dumping the flaming pile on the desk. I have no need of it anymore and I do not wish others to read it. It could be termed seditious, particularly given that I wish to survive my forthcoming confrontation with Jaegerstass. I have no doubt that it will be a confrontation. The General Doktor... he is the General Doktor. In his eyes I am no more than a successful experiment, practically a slave.

Reaching out to the Second Cohort, I find them on guard duty in the upper courtyard which is an inconvenient coincidence as I know the General Doktor is down in the vast unholy cavern where the portal is located. I cannot recall my soldiers without arousing suspicion.

#I would suggest you wait until the Second Cohort is more readily available to assist you.#

I disagree. I want to speak to General Doktor Jaegerstass man to man without the implied threat of my cohort.

#It's your funeral. And mine.#

As I leave my small cell, I become aware that I am more comfortable with my body of steel now than I have ever been previously. My machine intelligence must have spoken some truth regarding my adaptation to the armour. I wonder if my fellow Stürmgard have adapted as fully.

I ease through the narrow corridors and doorways, pausing now and again to let the occasional fearful duo of guards or castle staff past. They seem so small and delicate to me now. The castle itself is large, so large that only a small percentage of it is inhabited or utilised for any purpose. As a result the journey is quiet and unopposed.

In short time I find myself on the balcony overlooking the enormous underground chamber once again, the portal gate an oval of sparking structure encasing a calm opaque fog. Robots stood around the enclosing raised circle on the floor, hunched over like arthritic giants, their cannon at the ready. The generators hummed quietly away, centres in the storms of human activity that surged around them. I felt my eyes click slightly as they zoomed and focussed on the figures below. Thick bundles of cables wound across the sandy floor, pushed and rolled by many engineers to appropriate places. Other engineers stood around three large structures, each from which protruded a quartet of insulation pylons. Towards the rear of the cavern, a cohort of black armoured Stürmgard stood guard around the slight figure of General Doktor Jaegerstass, his bald head shining in the array of lights bathing the cavern in cold white, the oak leaves on his lapel winking as he moved his head. He simply stood there, watching, his eyes slowly scanning the hive of activity, missing nothing.

I continued to watch as I made my way down the wide, worn steps of the stone staircase. A slight man he may be but Jaegerstass emanated absolute authority, an authority that I was prepared to challenge. Me. An SS private.

#SS private no longer# chided my conscience. #A Stürmgard kommandant! Remember that. And I'm here too.#

Whispering lies into my ear day and night.

All too quickly I found myself standing in front of General Doktor Jaegerstass. As is normal, I looked down on the man from a height but despite the physical difference, I felt small, like a child facing an adult. His protective unit were taking no chances, their black chitinous armour drinking in light as they swivelled to cover me with unfamiliar weapons. Whether it was my nervousness or the colour of their armour but I found it difficult to focus on them as they merged with the shadows. My conscience muttered at my shoulder, an unwanted distraction.

"Ja?" Jaegerstass asked impatiently, his voice crisp.

"General Doktor Jaegerstass, I have some information regarding Neu Erde that you will find of interest." My own voice was hoarse and cracked. I'd turned off my external speakers.

"I will?" His eyes bored into mine, unblinking. "Why did you not inform me of your intelligence immediately on your return from Neu Erde?"

The second question caught me off guard with its distinctly double meaning and I stuttered to silence.

"Well?" The question snapped at me with almost physical force. Jaegerstass was not a man who was used to being kept waiting.

"Sir, I was overwhelmed by the implications of what I found. The shock was so much that I had to take time to contemplate what I had seen and run diagnostics to assure myself that my visual units had not failed."

#Oh bravo! Bravo! Excellently covered!#

I continued. "On a recovery mission to Site Loki, I discovered a mausoleum dedicated to Der Fuhrer."

A thin eyebrow rose though whether in surprise or scepticism I was unable to tell from that otherwise impassive face.

"I can provide videographic evidence," I continued laboriously. "Neu Erde is not Neu Erde. It is Erde in a future time. And I have discovered that the holocaust that resulted in the death of Erde was caused by this portal exploding in about thirty years time."

A smile quirked the corners of Jaegerstass's mouth. "Thirty years time, eh? I did not know that. That is extremely good news! I had a dire suspicion that the explosion may have happened today as a result of the upgrading of the portal that is being undertaken."

"You... you knew?"

"Of course I knew. It is my job to know things. Do you really think that I have not read the documents that we have retrieved from Neu Erde?"

"Documents?" I repeat stupidly.

"Swathes of books and paperwork that survived the holocaust, as you called it. Thank you for bringing your find to my attention. I am sure that the mausoleum of the first Fuhrer will receive the attention it deserves."

I simply stood there, shocked into immobility.

"Your audience is over. Report to your duties now Stürmgard," said Jaegerstass.

"But what about the portal? Will you not allow it to collapse?"

"To what end?" General Doktor Jaegerstass said "The future Erde is far away. It is not for us to worry about the future. That is for the generations of tomorrow who, armed with the knowledge we can give them, will survive and thrive away from Erde. Today we will conquer Erde for the Reich!"

His eyes glimmer with zeal and ambition. A madness shines forth as well, eager yet jittery.

#Kill him and destroy the time portal yourself. It's the only way!#

Nein. I am an SS soldier of the Reich. I must obey my superiors. I am firm in my resolve. Despite my frustrations I will not betray the Reich or Der Fuhrer.

#So much for saving the world! You capitulate at the first hurdle!#

Be quiet dumbkopf. I cannot feel the signatures of the Stürmgard or robots around the portal. It is as if my communications are being blocked. Do you have any doubt that I will be cut down the second I take a step out of place?

#Hmmm... What have we here? Ahhh... You are not being blocked but the control protocols are different. The Blitzsoldats and automata surrounding Jaegerstass must be part of a different army group. Unexpected but not a surprise. Der Fuhrer's mausoleum was guarded by several hundred inanimate Blitzsoldats, more than enough for a couple of army groups.#

I salute smartly as the voice on my shoulder rambles on.

I have a plan.

For the first time in so long that I cannot remember

For the first time in so long that I cannot remember, I feel the mind numbing, crushing weight of loneliness. I am of the SS, I am Stürmgard, and I disgust myself at being so weak yet at the same time I am not stupid enough to know that my attempts to control my emotions are futile. I am locked in this armoured cage, my mind and memories intact, unable to feel anything I touch, never once again able to taste the wonderful Bavarian beer of home nor the sauerkraut that Hans the butcher produces specially for the Oktoberfest. My friends and family will not recognise me, and if, by some wondrous miracle they did, I have little doubt that they would not accept me as the person I once was. My comrades are little more than mindless drones, ants scuttling around to satisfy the whims and commands of their overlord. I have nothing. Despair crushes me with her soft smothering hand, pushing down on me, the gentle dark fog of misery seeping into every corner of my consciousness.

#Steady on lad. There's no need for all these dire thoughts. If you're struggling to cope then I can prepare a concoction for you, a happy pill if you like.#

I do not like drugs whether medical or otherwise. They indicate a weakness of the mind and body. Yet I fleetingly consider responding with an affirmative. Instead, I said, I do not expect you to understand.

The white noise of laughter, sharp with scorn. #I understand you far better than you think. At least you still have control of your own life no matter how emasculated you feel. Me? I'm just along for the ride, forced to look where you look, to go where you go, trapped in your mind completely unable to communicate with anyone other than you. Did you ever think of that?#

I admit I had not but even having company in my black cube of depression did not alleviate my pain.

#It's probably the weather that's getting you down. Chin up.#

Accentuating the observation, the fog swirled dramatically and the light seemed to fade even further. If I had not switched to my infra red vision I would not be to see a thing. Even with my enhanced vision, the reinforced Second Cohort was only a collection of red smears against the cold and stark mountainside as we traversed the vegetation free landscape towards our goal; the ruined castle perched above us upon the peak of this Carpathian mountain.

As suddenly as it had appeared, the thick mist disappeared to reveal the jagged and broken towers of the castle; crumbling black teeth piercing the bruised purple of a darkening sky. Bats skittered and swirled around the foreboding fortress.

#It looks like Castle Dracula. That'll cheer you up.#

Is that its name?

#Have you ever read any books apart from Mein Kampf?#

I struggled to recall. I must have done so at school but the memories slipped away from the gaze of my mind's eye.

#Jaegerstass said that there's an Atlantean relic in there. They got about, those Atlanteans.#

I pushed aside my depression and focussed on the matter at hand. I was a soldier and my mission came first. I could not detect any movement, other than that of the Second Cohort as they silently secured the site, and the bats. We had beaten the Ahnenerbe to the castle after all. It disturbed me that I was in apparent competition with my fellow comrades of the Reich. Were we not all working together for the greater good of the Fatherland?

#There's nothing like a bit of unfriendly rivalry and internal party politics to warm the cockles of your heart.#

The wind screamed with laughter as I raced towards the ruins, leaping over ridges and chasms, playful gusts trying to toss me down the mountainside to break on the hidden crags and boulders far below.

#Never mind. We've a straight forward job here. Jaegerstass told us there was a chamber down in the dungeons where the relic should be.#

Am I able to scan for the relic?

#You're getting used to your fancy bits and bobs, aren't you?#

I could not prevent a smile crossing my face at that. It felt very strange. I could not remember the last time I had smiled at anything, certainly I found very little amusing now.

#To answer your question, yes you can scan for the relic. Hold on a second...#

While I waited, I directed the Second Cohort to form a defensive perimeter. I did not believe we would face any opposition in this extremely isolated location but unease prickled and poked at me. The Ahnenerbe was a very powerful branch of the SS whose tentacles stretched far and wide across the globe. They would not be far behind us.

#Ah there it is. Through the gatehouse, across the courtyard to the left, down the steps, left, straight on, right, down, left, right, voila.#

A three dimensional map hove into view with the route marked by a transparent orange line. I set off immediately, my increasing unease pushing me urgently along. Whether it was the deepening shadows, the bats fluttering from every nook and cranny, the possible arrival of the Ahnenerbe or all three, I felt jittery. The sooner I was out of here, the better.

The castle was old, the stones crumbling and weather worn, and covered in dank, dripping slime. Twice I nearly lost my footing - metal hooves, slime and crumbling stone do not make for sure-footedness. There were no doors to block my way as they had rotted away so long ago that not even their hinges remained. The only obstacle I faced was the cramped low ceilinged corridors that I barely managed to scrape through. Guided by the map, I quickly reached a rusted gate, the ancient metalwork of which was no match for my augmented strength not that I would have needed it.

Even with my light enhancing vision I struggled to see anything in the pitch darkness of this hole. The relic sat on a small stone bower and was a disappointment. I was expecting... well I did not know what to expect but certainly the elongated helmet did not quite have the aura of ancient Atlantis. It was covered in dirt and slime dripped over and through the elongated oval eye sockets. Carefully I wiped some of the grime away to reveal the plain unadorned yet also uncorroded metal beneath. Wide yet delicate cheek guards arced gracefully to meet at the point where a thin man's chin would be. A face piece covered the eyes and nose and hinted at an unearthly straight, thin nose and slanted eyes.

#A fine piece of work#

It was but it was just a helmet, a piece of armour of little use in the modern warfare of the 1940s. To my untutored eyes it was not worth the effort expended to gain possession of it.

#To my far older and experienced eyes, I agree. It's a fine piece of work as I said and it may surprise you to hear that it will stop anything short of a cannon round but no, it's not been worth... Hold on... We have hostiles on an inbound trajectory!#

Was ist das?

#Bad guys. Naughty people that likely want to kill us. They're on their way to the castle.#

Ahnenerbe?

#Your guess is as good as mine but who else could it be?#

I patched into Four's video feed, a view straight from his own eyes. It was completely dark outside now and only the pale light from a newly risen gibbous moon prevented total darkness. Four was perched in the remains of one of the towers facing our initial approach which provided him with an excellent view of the armoured zeppelin that was disgorging two squads of supersoldier beasts.

Scheiss. Definitely the Ahnenerbe. Only the Ahnenerbe used supersoldiers in this sort of quantity. All that was needed now to really ruin my day was...

#Great. Absolutely brilliant. Three Acolytes of Thule and their khadrae pets. It's been a while since I've killed some of those murdering bastards but I'd rather not meet them while holed up in the head of a green rookie.#

I bridled at the barbed observation, even as I shivered at the hisses and screeches from the khadrae. This was only the second time I'd ever seen the creatures and the first from close up. Their sinuous movements and serpentine hissing was unnerving. I licked my suddenly dry lips.

What makes you think they'll attack us? We're both on the same side.

#Theoretically, yes. I think you'll find the reality to be quite different. The Ahnenerbe prefer to be the sole benefactors of Atlantean technology and you are standing in their way. I wouldn't get your hopes up for a peaceful resolution.#

As I made my way back to the courtyard, my second in command stepped forward to reveal himself to the approaching mass. In an instant, eldritch green fire enveloped the acolytes as they pulled on their weird power to hurl the Fuhrer knows what at him, their khadrae screaming hatred and hauling on invisible leashes. The supersoldiers ground to halt with a rumble of guttural growls of confusion, raising their machine guns that were so crudely bolted and welded to their arms.

He never even had the chance to say a word before a beam of dazzling emerald played over him, eliciting a pained shout that crackled flatly from the hidden speakers on his armour. I had seen those beams disintegrate Tiger tanks so I was astonished to see Two lift his MG46 and return fire while limping backwards in retreat. Machine guns crackled from beyond as the supersoldiers took their cue from the acolytes, their shots sparking aimlessly across the ancient stonework, one or two spakking off Two's armour.

I didn't even have to issue an order, or perhaps it was an instinctive command much as I would clench my fist without having to think about it. Whatever it was, my cohort immediately returned fire, the large heavy calibre bullets sounding a drum roll of death as they exited the Stürmgard's triple barrelled machine guns. Khadrae screamed as their master fell under a withering hail of shells with his left arm blazing a deadly beam across old walls which wept treacle tears of pain. The beam flared once before dying as the acolyte's arm exploded from his body in a spray of barely seen blood and glittering shrapnel. The acolyte's sword was driven into the ground up to the hilt as he tried to use it to push himself upright again. His task proved pointless as his helmet disintegrated in a horizontal fountain of blood, bone and gristle.

As I watched, I let out an involuntary yell of pain as something stabbed through my head. For a second I thought I had been shot and my short time on Earth was at an end.

#Your number two has kicked the bucket I'm afraid. You felt some feedback from his death but I was able to filter the worst of it out. One of the disadvantages of your close integration with your squad.#

I saw Two finally fall under the gaze of two of those despicable eye searing beams. Raising my gun, I sprang forward across the courtyard, targeting reticules crowding my vision as the khadrae surged forward, a tidal wave of teeth and claws that glittered in the moonlight.

From their vantage points in the castle, my cohort exchanged fire with the remaining two acolytes and supersoldiers.

Still patched into Four's video feed, I saw two blinding green bars reach up to find him. For a second I felt his armour melt and the molten metal fill his eye sockets and mouth before the feedback was cut. I staggered as another bolt of pain speared me. My men! They were being slaughtered! I must save them!

Distracted by the death pains of Four, I was caught unawares and was staggered again as a khadrae slammed into me with its claws pulled back like meathooks. Bone screeched against metal fibre mesh as the animal attempted to eviscerate me while simultaneously biting my head off. Slaver and drool dripped down my visor as serrated teeth scratched across it. I had an odious view down a khadrae's gullet. My nose wrinkled despite the isolating faceplate protecting me from both teeth and reeking breath. I rammed my hand into the khadrae's mouth, gripped its jaw and smashed its skull against the cobbles, splattering grey brain and white skull across the ground. Another khadrae careered into me then another and another. Alone they would be a pitiful opponent for me but as a pack they were far more deadly. Under the repeated impacts I fell backwards on to the cobblestones and felt my gun slide away from my grasp. The khadrae scraped and worried away at my armour.

#Get the khadrae off you now before they find the weak spots in your armour and start cutting. Now! NOW!#

The khadrae were many but I was strong. And still armed. Blades sprang out to line my vambraces and gauntlets as I heaved aside the kahadrae worrying my arms. I threw two punches at the single khadrae standing on my chest, both of which connected with satisfying cracks as bone caved beneath the force of the blows which sent the wounded khadrae scurrying away into the darkness, squealing pitifully.

I was dimly aware that Eight was engaged in hand to hand combat with several supersoldiers who had sneaked in through a previously unnoticed breach in the castle walls. He was holding his own despite the odds.

As I sat up, I almost screamed as I felt more pain spear its way through my head, powerful, jagged and almost physical. Spots swam in front of my eyes. I had no stomach yet an old instinctive memory told me that bile was rising.

#Sorry. I can't block the death feedback completely. Seven and Nine gone.#

My men! Fury seized me in a blazing hot grip. It wasn't red unthinking rage but clear and white. As I kicked the remaining three khadrae off me and cast them back into the seething mass that held back watching me with their bat like clicks and squeals, I felt an odd sense of deja vu creep across me as if I had fought these foul animals before. They were held back no doubt by their masters' whim, and likely, their masters' desire for a prisoner to interrogate. I would never be taken prisoner. Ever. I do not surrender. I do not give in. I do not fall to the enemy. Victory or death.

Hastily I retrieved my gun, wincing (but only wincing this time) as Six died, blown apart by an eerily accurate salvo of cannon fire emanating from the zeppelin.

#There will be acolytes aboard the zeppelin using their witch powers to locate the Stürmgard and direct the cannon fire. End this now!#

Without thought I opened fire as I ran forwards, my gun moving almost of its own accord as I cycled through the multiple glowing orange targeting reticules that lined up across my sight. The slight bodies of the khadrae simply exploded as my shots cratered their skin, liquifying muscle, tissue and internal organs before bursting through to repeat the process once maybe twice more. Fire, adjust aim, fire, adjust aim, fire, repeat, repeat, repeat. It was as if I was not in complete control of myself.

#Watch out!#

A reticule blazed red and I swivelled to my left as a sparkling longsword slashed down towards me, missing by barely a hands breath, so close that electrical arcs from the sword earthed themselves on me.

A blade 60 centimetres long sprang out from my right gauntlet as I continued my spin, pirouetting like a ballet dancer as I raised the blade and delivered a blow to the back of the acolyte's neck. The blade sliced through the man's armour with an ease that caught me totally by surprise and I almost lost my balance. A spray of red on my blade was the only sign of my attack for several seconds. The sounds of the battlefield faded to silence as if everyone and everything was watching with bated breath. The acolyte lurched forward a single step before his head slowly detached itself from his shoulders and, almost in slow motion, fell to the ground with a thud before rolling twice over. Equally slowly, the beheaded body followed like a felled tree crashing to the ground with a clang as the cast metal hit rock. As if the ringing sound was a signal, half the khadrae raised their heads and unleashed a long and painful howl that rent my soul.

#A soul? An SS beast like you? You're no better than the khadrae. A animal.# I scowled at the little voice that lived in my head.

Mein kameraden did not miss the opportunity. From various points along the castle wall and the broken tooth towers, jagged fire blazed yellow and red, bright in the darkness. The khadrae fell like the proverbial chaff in the wind. Their bright blue blood filled the air like an ocean spray.

Cannon fire cracked out once more and the rain of fire from the castle slackened as clouds of flame enveloped precise sections. A dull headache. My men! Rage filled me. Anger like I had not known before coursed through my body. A red mist descended in front of my eyes. The zeppelin must be destroyed. All these Ahnenerbe vermin must die!

#There's... there's no time for that. Stay calm. Concentrate.#

A cocktail of drugs washed over me in a cleansing wave killing the fire that burned. However, deep down, I could feel the embers still glowing.

An acolyte staggered drunkenly across my field of vision with his sword carelessly slicing the air into ribbons, the man himself enveloped in eldritch green thorns. I stepped around his sword and brought my fist down on his armoured head to squash the horns, helmet and head within equally flat with a satisfying squelch.

#The zeppelin cargo bay doors have been left wide open. The Ahnenerbe weren't expecting opposition, careless bunch that they are. Make them pay for their carelessness!#

Gentle curves of bright tracer bullets tracked me as I sprinted across the barren rock, bright sparks lighting my wake. I was too fast for the gunners who had spotted me. Too fast by far. Within seconds I had rushed into the cavernous hold of this armoured beast and cut down a few startled Ahnenerbe soldiers with a few brief shots. Even now I do not feel any remorse for the killing of my fellow Germans. They murdered my men without a second thought. I was the consequence that they must face.

The interior of the airship reeked of dark magicks and the air was tainted by a dark haze that clouded my senses and played tricks on my eyes. Shadows danced and flickered around the hold despite the steadily burning lights along the bulkheads.

I hesitated, blinking as I automatically tracked the shifting ragged shapes.

#There's nothing there. The Thule Cult sorcerers are playing tricks on you.#

A schematic of the zeppelin appeared in front of me.

#The gasbags are above us, up those steps to your right. A few punctures here and there will bring the zeppelin crashing down to earth.#

Incendiary shots will ignite them. A funeral pyre is a far better way to dispose of these people.

#If they were full of hydrogen then yes but these 'modern' airships are kept aloft by helium which is far less combustible.#

I was not satisfied. I did not want any survivors.

Distracted as I was, I did not see my assailant. The first blow jarred every bone in my body or at least it felt it should have done, and I fell against a stack of wooden packing crates which smashed into shards and splinters. The grim patchwork face of a supersoldier swam before my eyes before an iron boot clanged into my side and sent me scraping a sparking wake across the hold.

#No damage. Your armour is impregnable to this sort of rough stuff but any more of this and something's going to come loose... Look out!#

I turned on to my side just in time to avoid a flying knee drop form the supersoldier. Obviously this one wasn't the average slab of meat.

Jabbing my elbow towards the misshapen face, I rolled around and scissored my legs around the off balanced half man and straightened them before it could respond. I felt rather than heard the crack, and the supersoldier went limp, a sudden deadweight across my legs that I quickly kicked off.

I sprang to my feet, ears straining as I listened for any further surprise attacks. The shifting shadows made me doubt the veracity of my own eyes. I was embarrassed to have been caught out like an amateur...

#And so you should be.#

It was you that told me there was nothing about! Silence.

Silence from my little voice but intermittent gunfire echoed from outside along with eerie calls from the surviving khadrae. Nothing stirred in the hold. The atmosphere was heavy with expectancy.

#I'm detecting radio transmissions form the zeppelin. You've got them all riled up, son. They've no idea who or what you are... They're not running scared but someone is a tad annoyed at losing half his force. Shame that.#

I paused but only for a moment. What I thought was fear was the anticipation of the battle to come. I smiled. And I had the sensation of someone at my shoulder smiling too. Perhaps my guardian angel.

#I've located the bridge. Follow the yellow brick road.#

Even as I puzzled over the obscure reference, a skeletal blue depiction of the zeppelin infrastructure floated in front of me with a glowing yellow route marked out against it.

#We've got some incoming bad guys too. Be prepared!#

I grunted an irritated acknowledgement. I am Stürmgard. I am always prepared.

The bridge was to the fore of the zeppelin where the compartment was built into the nose which surprised me. I had always thought the bridge was part of the gondola slung beneath the gas containing envelope.

#They usually are but these armoured zeppelins of yours aren't your normal easily poppable run of the mill types. They still have gasbags but most of the staying aloft work is placed on the shoulders of low grade Thule Cult sorcerers.#

The Thule Cult has been eradicated from German society by order of the Fuhrer. There is no place for religion in the Nazi state.

#Yup, yup, uh huh. That's right. No place at all. Yet here we are...#

Sometimes the voice annoyed me intensely.

I flung myself up the wide ladder highlighted yellow into a corridor above the cargo bay and landed straight into a hailstorm of lead.

#Remember those bad guys?#

Yes, I responded testily as bullets pinged and whistled a cacophonous din as they met the superior metal alloy mesh that was my armoured body. The black uniformed soldiers with the red swastika and stylised pillars on their lapels were armed with the latest Sturmgewehr 44 assault rifles. I easily recognised the large automatic guns even though it was certainly the first time I recalled seeing them. I did not even look at the men as I gunned them down, my own weapon drowning out the stuttering gunfire of the inferior soldiers as flesh, blood and bone sprayed across the corridor floor and walls. They are beneath me. I am Stürmgard. I would not have wasted bullets on them but I was travelling in the opposite direction and did not wish to waste time. Turning to following the glowing yellow line ahead of me, I noted how dark and narrow the corridor was. The fug from the cargo bay persisted here, pooling beneath the few lamps that struggled against the oppressive darkness, the yellow light travelling nowhere near as far as it should have done. My optical enhancements struggled to penetrate the gloom and lines of static criss crossed my vision.

Whether it was down to dark arts or if the sorcerer's ink black cowl and robes simply camouflaged him, I don't know but the first time I saw him was when green fire enveloped his hands and he stepped out of the shadows to grasp my left forearm.

I will not deny I was overconfident but I was also curious. What did one of these legendary Thule Cult sorcerers look like? His face was shadowed beneath the cowl with only the stub of a pure white chin visible, luminous in the green fire. Slowly, in a series of jerky movements that increased my unease with each one, he raised his face to look at me. I recoiled at the rictus grin of filed teeth stretched across the lipless bone coloured face. His nose was barely there, seemingly having rotten away but it was his eyes that disturbed me most. Or rather his lack of them. Ragged sockets had been crudely stitched over with thread that had once been white but was now the colour of a scabbed wound. A serpent's tongue flickered out from his mouth tasting the air.

I recoiled in horror but was astonished to find I could not pull away from his seemingly light grip on my arm. The sorcerer hissed. I blinked as his free arm jerked back never appearing to move between the positions at which it materialised. His hand opened to reveal a cadaverous palm and long thin fingers ending in equally thin curved nails. Talons almost. Then his palm was suddenly against my breast plate, there was a dazzling emerald flash and I was flying backwards down the corridor, my vision flashing red in between lines of crackling static.

#Ye Gods! He can't half punch above his weight! You've got multiple system failures but nothing I can't deal with. However, a couple of more blows like that and it's lights out for us.#

A targeting reticule faded in and out over the shadowy figure before juddering out of sight as my shoulder hit an exposed girder and I crashed to the floor. My head was full of buzzing and pops and I had trouble focussing my attention on the slight, fuzzy figure that seemed to be floating towards me. Where was my aiming reticule? I couldn't shoot without knowing where I was shooting at!

#You don't need an automatic targeting system. Just point your gun and shoot the bugger!#

I frowned without feeling my face move in empathy. Of course. My gun bucked and kicked as I pulled the trigger, the ammunition belt clattering out from its hopper as it fed the death dealing device. Still the figure in its clouds of darkness and green lightning came onwards behind a transparent shield of green that cracked where my shots hit it.

What do I do? What do I do? I couldn't think as fear grasped me with his chilly embrace. The eyeless corpse thing grinned wider as his sleeves fell to expose almost transparent white skin that crawled with silver tattoos. The very act of looking at the warped symbols caused my throat to constrict and my head to pound with pain. Blue and green lightning flickered around the elongated fingers. What do I do? I whimpered.

#Pull yourself together soldier! I always knew you SS bastards were soft! No British grit in you, that's your problem! When in doubt, a swift application of physical violence will solve most problems. Get on your feet now!#

The embers flared and the heat of rage fill me again and cast out the cold hands of fear. Fastening my gun to my back, I clambered to my feet, noting with satisfaction the twitch of surprise that crossed the sorcerer's face as he stopped.

I took a step towards the thing and suddenly I was enveloped in arcing bolts of pain. Pain that I had never felt before, and hope I never will feel again, drove me to my knees screaming. Pain was all I could feel. Pain was all I could see. Pain was all I could hear. My nose filled with the stench of electrical burning and I tasted blood as I bit my tongue in between screams.

But I do not give in. I do NOT give in. Never. Ever. Ever. Victory or death. Victory. Pain. Victory.

I could not concentrate. I just did. Lift my leg. Put my foot down on the floor. Rise. Fight the pain. Stand. Fight the pain. I could not see anything except impossibly bright jagged lines that earthed themselves on me. Lift leg. Put foot down. Repeat with other leg. Repeat. Move towards the source of the pain. He was there in front of me, his face no longer emblazoned with that smile of death. If he still had eyes I know that I would have seen fear in them. My right hand enveloped his head and I squeezed. There was nothing to feel. His skull simply gave way beneath the pressure I exerted as I crushed his loathsome head. Blood and matter seeped out from between my fingers as the cloak of shadows shuddered once and disappeared to leave behind a pathetically thin man in a black robe, his body twitching and jerking as it responded to the final commands from its dead brain.

The pain ceased leaving behind a void. A void through which I could see clearly. I am a machine. I locate a target. I kill. Locate. Kill. Locate. Kill. Again and again and again. Nothing can stand against me. I am a god machine. That is all I am. I have no purpose other than to locate and destroy the enemies of the Reich.

#Such as the Ahnenerbe. 'God machine'. Good grief. Back in the real world, the sorcerers' lair is just ahead. Brace yourself son. This won't be pretty.#

I thought we were going to the bridge?

#We are.#

As I stepped over the emaciated body, I heard a hum that reminded me of a radio tuned into a station that has not yet started broadcasting. The hum increased in intensity the further I progressed towards the bridge and the static across my eyes got worse. I could see chaotically flickering light ahead around a sharp corner.

#My advice to you is to open fire on anything that moves. If we had grenades I'd be telling you chuck them all in to the bridge. Keep moving. Don't be a sitting duck.#

I unholstered my gun, finding reassurance in its physical mass. I stepped around the corner into the bridge and stopped dead. What was once a bridge was now a slaughter house. A decapitated body was tied to the ship's wheel, blood draining into a bucket underneath the upended carcass. Darkness clouded the room, blacker than the night that could be barely seen out of blood flecked windows. Flayed bodies were crudely nailed to the wood panelled walls, exposed muscle and organs glistening in the dim and flickering light, the recipients of the torture still screaming and moaning in agony.

The darkness seemed to coalesce into three human forms or perhaps they had always been there but I had not noticed them. I could not move. Too many times on this mission I have been struck immobile with horror but I defy any man to have done otherwise.

With deceptive slowness a whip seemingly made of fire lashed out towards me and scoured my breastplate leaving behind smoking scars.

#Remember your men! Remember they died because of the creatures before you. God damn you! Don't just stand there you fool!#

Laughter mocked me. Laughter shot through with pain and madness. It came from one of the bodies nailed to the walls. I could see the man's lungs inflate and deflate as he laughed and then cried tears that I do not doubt burned as they rolled down his raw face. I retched. This was just so completely wrong. This was not what the Third Reich fought for. Nein. This was wrong. Just totally wrong. No man deserved to be tortured in such a way.

I opened fire only to feel dismay as the bullets passed through the shadowy forms.

#Ah hah! Look what I've found!#

The static cleared from my vision as a green band sparked downwards, removing all the darkness from the room and leaving behind only three luminous beings at the centre. Thick tentacles of green writhed out from them and embedded themselves in the now faint forms so crudely attached to the walls.

#Do you understand what you're seeing?#

I did not and I had no time to guess.

#The sorcerers are drawing their power from the sacrifices. Remove the sacrifices and you remove their power.#

I didn't hesitate. In a way I was thankful that I was able to end their suffering. I raked the walls with gunfire, wood, flesh and bone exploding alike. The iron scent of blood mixed with the sweet smell of the wood. The three forms fell to their knees screaming as the source of their power was wrenched away. Gut. I hoped they were suffering. Outside in the night, I saw the mountain rear up against the zeppelin and crash into the comparatively small machine. I grunted as I fell forward with the impact but leapt to my feet straight away. I had things to do.

The emerald glow surrounding the three sorcerers had disappeared leaving behind three pathetic wailing little men. I ignored them as I faced the first lolling red body on the wall next to me. I carefully pulled out the nails that pierced the man's arms and laid the body on the floor. I noted with disgust the shreds of skin, urine and shit that lay beneath the man but he was dead now and there was nowhere else to put him. I did not think he would care much I repeated the process with the second, third, fourth, fifth and sixth bodies, my chest contracting as I tried to imagine the pain they had gone through. The seventh body was the one tied to the wheel which I cut down and also laid to rest as best I could in the circumstances.

The sorcerers had not moved from their collective crying heap. I sneered. Pathetic, snivelling, bullying vermin. Germany was better than them.

I picked one of them up by the arm and lifted him into the air. He tried to attack me but I tightened my grip slightly and he squealed loudly. I held him against the wall, picked up a nail and pushed it through his wrist joint. A second nail went through his opposite wrist. He continued squealing and writhed in pain so I thought I had better put several more nails into him just to make sure he didn't rip free. His screams had subsided to whimpers by the time I put the eighth and last nail through his ankle.

I ignored the stark terror on the thin faces of the remaining two sorcerers just as they had no doubt ignored the terror and pain on the faces of their many victims. One of them tried to run so I snapped his leg beneath my hoof. I pinned the two men up on the walls as if they were butterflies or moths.

I felt no satisfaction as I viewed my handiwork.

#That's good. You are not like them.#

I had my revenge I supposed. Yet I felt nothing. I felt empty as if there was a black hole within me and nothing could fill it or ever would. My men were all dead, sacrificed for nothing, killed to satisfy a madman's whim. I could not believe that these... these... sorcerers (I could not use the word 'men') are allowed to practice what they do in a nation like Germany.

#A nation like Germany. Where you shoot Jewish children for sport.#

I struggled with the whirlpool of emotions and memories that flooded across my mind's eye. I could see myself in the third person carefully tracking the reckless and desperate sprint of a grubby dark haired, dark eyed child clad in rags with a Star of David crudely daubed on her back. I saw myself fire and the bullet speed across the open ground before striking the child between the shoulder blades. I saw myself smile with satisfaction and make a mark on a notebook. I saw the child turn over, pain twisting her face as blood bubbled raggedly from her lips, once, twice and then the light went out in her eyes. This was me. This is who I am. I groaned. It was wrong. It was not... human. This is who I was not who I am. I am a soldier. A soldier protects the realm... protects the Reich and its people. A soldier does not murder like these wizards.

A blue dot began to pulse softly on my visor. My extraction call.

#I've attempted to contact the rest of the Stürmgard. There are no survivors.#

It was there and then that I made my decision. I had one more mission before I returned to Schloss Schwabenstein.

The End

The MI6 listening post sat in the lee of the sharp toothed Swiss mountain, but despite its sheltered location the wind still battered snow against the thin panes of glass which rattled in their frames against the equally thin wooden walls. Nominally, the lonely hut was a bothy, a respite for tired mountaineers to rest and seek shelter from the bad weather that frequently scoured the Alps. The Swiss would have a fit if they knew what the British had hidden under it...

Schiehallion, Macrihanish, Listening Post 22; underground bases and command centres all, though Captain Brian Drennan would be the first to admit that Listening Post 22 was significantly smaller than either of the two vast bases. Sleeping quarters for six, a small canteen cum kitchen, a fairly large lounge with well stocked bookshelves (essential when cooped up for several months) and finally, the glittering radio and computational engine room. Currently Listening Post 22 was home to radio operators Claire Hale, Tina Agnew and Gillian Erskine, the trio who were sitting with headphones on, their pencils scratching across pads of paper as they intercepted German radio transmissions.

Captain Drennan looked around the radio room, eyes narrowing in annoyance. Was McEvoy bunking off once again? No, there he was, under one of the computational engines, swearing quietly under his breath as he surveyed a tangled fistful of wires and cabling. That particular computational engine had been giving them problems all week - something to do with the new high speed tape devices apparently. McEvoy had been flown in specially to fix the issue and to give all the other engines a poke, a prod and a dash of oil; whatever it was these engineer chaps did to get the best out of their charges. The Germans had been tinkering with their Enigma codes again. Prior to last week, the banks of computational engines had coped admirably with any changes in the ciphers and after a day or two of rumination they were back to decoding the Enigma messages pretty much

72

instantaneously within an hour or two of their interception. However, four days ago, the communications had once again become indecipherable and had remained so. Drennan drummed his fingers on the arm of his chair, drawing irritated glances from the three women which he duly ignored. He didn't agree with women being out here at the cutting edge of intelligence gathering but he would not deny that they had some of the best ears in the business. Fine looking women too but he didn't dwell on that.

The Captain pondered the uncrackable codes. The Nazis could not possibly have achieved a technological advantage over British ingenuity. Surely? His inner ear tickled as it sometimes did from the constant scratch scratch of pencils on paper. It was a relatively quiet day. He'd filed several reports with London - just the standard radio chatter regarding troop deployments throughout the Third Reich. Certainly nothing of note. The Nazis had no suspicions whatsoever about the coming invasion. They seemed to think the stalemate would continue indefinitely while they tootled around Europe undermining and annexing as they went. Hah! Old Hitler was in for a shock! Drennan glanced at the calendar on his desk, checking the date against the automatic calendar on the wall. It was easy to lose track of time down in this sunless man made cave. Yes. As he'd thought, D-Day was only sixteen days away.

Scritch scratch, a short cough and a clearing of a throat. Equipment hummed sedately, tapes whirred quietly away occasionally clicking and clacking in their large drive units. McEvoy mumbled away to himself as he joined cables together and neatly stashed them away. The quiet sounds were soporific and not for the first time, Drennan found himself dropping off into the land of Nod.

He jerked awake. Something was wrong. The equipment hummed away as normal. No scritch scratch.

"What's the problem?" he asked of the three radio operators as he stood up and walked over to where they sat in front of their equipment, flicking switches and turning dials as they tried to tune into particular frequencies.

Agnew removed her headphones and examined them, a puzzled expression creasing her round face.

"I'm not getting anything at all," she said as she tapped the earpieces in turn before holding the pair to her right ear while her fingers flew across the dials in front of her. "No, nothing. Here, have a listen."

Drennan took the proffered headphones and held them to his ear. Sure enough there wasn't a squeak from them, nor a hiss or crackle as would be expected. He flicked the tuning dial round to a frequency he knew the Wehrmacht Fourth Army was using to co-ordinate anti partisan operations in Austro-Hungary. Nothing.

"Are the headphones working?" he asked Agnew.

"My headphones are dead as well," said Hale before Agnew could say anything.

"I'm not getting anything through mine either," added Erskine.

"Oh hell," said McEvoy, his Scots brogue incongruous in a room full of familiar English accents.

Drennan reached the same conclusion a second later. "Damn. We're being jammed."

"But they can't jam us..." Erskine started before realisation dawned. She put her hand to her mouth, eyes wide.

"The Nazis can't jam us unless they know we're here," Captain Drennan finished for her. He leapt the short distance to his desk and flipped up a metal cover to reveal a red button which he duly pressed.

"We're going into lockdown," he announced, unable to keep the tension out of his voice as the room reverberated to the wheeze and grind of pneumatic pistons pushing a huge slab of steel reinforced concrete over the entrance above, entombing them. "Break out the Stens Hale."

The Captain looked at McEvoy who swallowed nervously as he ran his hand over his thinning hair.

"We have to send a distress signal McEvoy, otherwise there's no rescue..."

The remainder of his sentence was cut off as a thud came from outside, echoing down the entrance corridor, quiet and distant but undeniably real.

"God damn them. Already?" breathed Drennan as his eyes flicked up to the televisual screens behind his desk. Three cameras were placed higher up the mountainside to allow remote observation of the rugged landscape surrounding the bothy. Normally they showed nothing more than bare rocks covered and uncovered by shifting snow. Normally. Drennan pushed his face right up to the middle monitor, trying to make out the shapes obscured by the snowstorm that was raging above them. What the hell was that?

"McEvoy! Do whatever you can get to get a message out!" Drennan barked.

Hale returned from the armoury, struggling with the awkward weight of five Sten submachine guns. McEvoy relieved her of one before sitting himself in front of one of the computational engines, his face sepulchral in the green glow from the flickering cathode ray screen. Keys clattered as his fingers flew across the keyboard. Like a concert pianist thought Drennan as he took a Sten from Hale and ratcheted the well oiled bolt back to load a bullet into the chamber.

"Damn nuisance this," he said to no one in particular. "This listening post has given us great intelligence. It'll be a real blow losing it. And the Swiss will go barmy when they find out."

He sat on his chair, leaning back and feeling the tension of moments ago leaving him. All they had to do now was sit tight. McEvoy would get an SOS out somehow - there were ways and means - and nothing could get through the feet thick concrete door that now protected them.

He smiled reassuringly at the radio operators. "The Stens are just a precaution. There's no need for them really. No need for them at all."

Clearing his throat, he looked around for a book he knew was somewhere on his desk. "Righty ho then. Sit down, have a cup of tea and by the time we're finished tea, rescue will be on the way. Nothing to worry about!"

"No pressure then!" chimed in McEvoy sarcastically.

Everyone knew the drill. Keep calm, carry on. They were all highly trained MI6 officers after all. Erskine pushed a loose strand of blonde hair behind her ear, slung her Sten over her shoulder and went off to the canteen. Five teas. Four with milk and sugar, one black with a touch of honey for the Captain. He was very avant garde.

Hale and Agnew sat together at a radio station.

"I wonder if we can get something out on the UHF band," Agnew said as she idly turned a few dials.

"The Osiris might pick it up," nodded Hale. "Captain, do you know where the Osiris is?"

The Osiris was one of the RAF's high altitude reconnaissance airships.

"It might be about," replied Drennan. "Give it a whirl. There's no harm in trying."

Thump. A long drawn out scraping. Silence. No one said anything but the room seemed to close in around them and the room appeared to be hotter, stifling. Drennan knew it was psychological but he couldn't help himself undoing his top button. He still couldn't make out anything on the television monitors. Just shapes moving in the snowstorm. Could be the abominable snowman has come to the Alps, he snorted.

"Captain, I can't get through to London!" called McEvoy. "Nothing at all. I can't break through the jamming."

McEvoy shook his head in frustration. "I've never seen jamming like this before. Normally you hear static but this is just nothing, as if our signals are being cancelled out completely. It's just not possible."

"Owwww!" Agnew dropped her headphones with a clatter, rubbing her ears as pain and surprise marred her usually smooth face. High pitched screeching and static squeals of varying pitches filled the radio room, emanating from Agnew's headphones.

Thump, thump, THUD. The pounding echoed, a drumroll of doom. All eyes fell on the narrow corridor that led up to the bothy and the concrete covered entrance. Drennan rose from his seat and peered into the darkness. Was that a chink of light he could see? Impossible. Absolutely impossible. It would take a tank to break through, and even then he would be bet against the tank. He swung the heavy metal corridor door shut and sealed it with a quick spin of the locking wheel. He wiped away sweat that dripped down his nose. There was no escape from Listening Post 22, no secret back door to run out of.

A tremendous crack made everyone jump, their hands automatically scrambling for their weapons. A shaft of light shone through the small rectangular window on the sealed door, its whiteness startling in the dark room of green and red lights. The entrance had been breached. Against all odds, the entrance had been breached. The light disappeared. The Nazi attack force was moving towards them.

"Defensive positions!" barked Drennan. "Fire at will! If it's a small force then we can take them out and head onto the mountains."

He heaved his desk over onto its side, scattering paper, pens and pencils across the floor. "Erskine! Forget the tea! Get down here at the double!"

The Captain dared a peek through the window. A gasp slipped past his lips as his eyes widened in shock, suddenly nerveless fingers fumbling the safety catch on his Sten.

With a clap like thunder, the door burst out from its frame like a cannon shell. Captain Drennan never knew what hit him as his body cracked and flattened against the flying slab of metal. Tina Agnew had no time to react either as the door and bloody remains of the captain smashed into her, crushing her legs and pelvis with audible snaps as she hit the bank of equipment. The pain was like a shadowy boulder rolling over her. She never regained consciousness before her life trickled out in streamers of red.

Despite being blinded by the sudden light, both Hale and McEvoy opened fire with stuttering Stens. Silver flashed and Hale's head was suddenly encased in a gauntleted fist. She continued firing even as she screamed under the mounting pressure, even as she felt her skull crack and splinters drove themselves into her brain. Her legs and arms spasmed as she was lifted into the air like a grotesque doll, her gun still spraying bullets. McEvoy had nowhere to run even if he hadn't been rooted to the spot with shock and terror. Hale's bullets hit him like a heavyweight boxer's punch except punches did not pull out a quarter pound of flesh nor did they liquidise internal organs. The engineer gasped as he felt the burn of stomach acid starting to eat its way through what remained of his insides. The dreadful pain was mercifully short as a massive fist swung round and ripped his head off in a spraying arc of dark crimson.

Gillian Erskine heard Captain Drennan shout for her and reached for her Sten which she had left on the tabletop. Before she had taken a step out from the canteen into the main corridor, a massive bang came from the radio room, rapid gunfire, Hale screamed, McEvoy gasped raggedly; it was a horrific crescendo of battle and pain interspersed with sharp cracks and crunches. Then silence.

White winter light shone along the corridor towards Erskine, casting shadows of cut onyx. Something creaked and hissed as it moved, a great shadow that eclipsed the wan light. A computational machine keyboard clattered to the floor. An irritating whine followed, a sound Erskine recognised as all the tape drives spinning together.

The MI6 officer licked her lips nervously as she quietly edged forward, her soft soled shoes noiseless on the rough floor. Carefully, so as to avoid any warning sounds, she eased the safety off the safety catch on her sub machine gun. A whiff of smoke tickled her nostrils. Lines creased her forehead as she recognised the acrid scent of overheating computational machines. She rubbed her nose to stifle an oncoming sneeze.

A figure knelt in front of the machines, outlined by baleful red lights, which stared accusingly at her - where were you when your friends died? A clear shot. She didn't hesitate. A tight burst of bullets caught the figure squarely on the chest. It didn't move. A clean kill, Erskine smiled grimly. She padded forward carefully. There had to be more soldiers... Her breath caught in her throat as she saw the ruined remains of her colleagues. Her friends. She could not prevent tears blurring her eyes. She never saw the blade that lanced through her right lung. Liquid burbled from her lips in painful gasps as she slipped to the floor, her strength leaving her with every wet gasp of air.

She realised her mistake as she focussed on the behemoth crouched next to a computational machine in front of her. It was a Nazi supersoldier but not one she had she ever seen before. Wrapped in close fitting plate armour, the contours did not hide the muscled bulk that must lie beneath. And it had a face! A normal human face most unlike that of the brutal, animalistic supersoldiers. Despite the deep pain in her chest, Erskine was curious. The supersoldier's left arm rested on the table with a short cable snaking out into where the keyboard had once been plugged. The serene face watched as green text danced and scrolled across the cathode ray tube.

"What are you doing?" she struggled to ask in German.

The cold face turned to her, its equally cold eyes like blue steel chips. It looked like an angel, Erskine's fevered imagination told her.

"I am supplying British Intelligence with the location of a rogue German advanced research division. It must be destroyed," the supersoldier responded in perfect though strangely accented English.

"W...Why?" Erskine grimaced. The pain was hot, burning her chest, yet her legs were cold, a numbness spreading from her feet. She couldn't feel her fingers.

"It must be stopped. The world will be destroyed if the research it is undertaking is not halted. The Third Reich will be annihilated by one of its own."

"Why not do it yourself?"

The supersoldier grunted. Whether it was a laugh or suppressed irritation, Erskine couldn't tell from the expressionless face.

"The Nazi hierarchy does not agree with my reasoning. It is blinded by greed and a lust for power. I will not let the Reich fall due to the short sightedness of the few."

The MI6 officer could see only blurs now. Warm lights of red and yellow blinked and faded, blinked and faded like a repeated sunset. The surprisingly soft voice was the only thing she could hear, filling her consciousness. Her breathing was shallow, no longer paining her. She struggled to see as metal creaked and the giant silver figure filled her failing vision.

"Who are you?" she whispered. Her head lolled onto her chest, eyes staring unseeing as her final breath whistled from her mouth.

He looked down on her dispassionately.

"I am Stefan Stahl."

#I am James Riley#